Boy of Heaven

Boy *of* Heaven

BY
Morris Hoffman

RESOURCE *Publications* · Eugene, Oregon

BOY OF HEAVEN

Resource Publications
An Imprint of Wipf and Stock Publishers
199 W. 8th Ave., Suite 3
Eugene, OR 97401

www.wipfandstock.com

PAPERBACK ISBN: 979-8-3852-4578-9
HARDCOVER ISBN: 979-8-3852-4579-6
EBOOK ISBN: 979-8-3852-4580-2

VERSION NUMBER 04/21/25

For Kate

Contents

Excerpt from Bonnard's *A Brief History of Milan* | viii

The Liturgical Year, annis Domini 1681–82 | ix

1 Carrots for the Stars | 1

2 Aquila | 10

3 His Feet | 19

4 The Stars and the Men | 29

5 The Twelfth Star | 39

6 The Masters and Signorie | 48

7 The Bishops and Archbishop | 55

8 Soldiers of the Black Fire | 63

9 Home | 71

In 1463, the Duke [Francesco I, founder of the Sforza dynasty] commissioned the construction of a small Dominican church and priory on the western outskirts of the City, and named it Santa Marie delle Grazie. It was completed in 1469. His son Ludovico made several restorations to the complex, intending its church to become his family's mausoleum. In 1495, as part of these restorations, Ludovico patronized the already famous Florentine master Leonardo DaVinci, who was to live in the City and complete a mural spanning the north wall of the priory's refectory. Leonardo chose as his subject for this dining hall mural Jesus's final meal on the evening before his crucifixion. The artist worked at his customary pace, in fits and starts separated by long interruptions, and to Ludovico's great dismay did not complete the mural until 1498.

Upon its completion, the The Last Supper was met with immediate and universal acclaim. It was the most copied painting for the next several centuries, and remains today one of the most copied pieces of art in all of human history. It turned tiny Santa Maria delle Grazie into an important cultural hub, contributing critically to the City's economic stability in the difficult years of the Italian Wars, as it suffered in the crossfire between the French and Spanish. The City may well have been spared some of the excesses of war simply because of the proximity of the great painting.

Its lasting cultural impact is all the more remarkable because the dry plaster on which it was painted began deteriorating within a few years after its completion, a process accelerated by the heat and moisture from the adjoining kitchen. By the time the Spanish took the City and the surrounding territories in 1535, the painting was compromised to the point of being virtually invisible. Indeed, it was so damaged that in 1652 the Dominican friars felt no compunction when they cut a door into the wall to connect the refectory with the kitchen, removing the near indiscernible image containing Jesus's feet, crossed under the table. The removed wall panel was never found, and was presumed destroyed.

Marcel Bonnard, A Brief History of Milan

The Liturgical Year

annis Domini 1681–82

The Temporale (Proper of Time)

Adventus	November 27
Feast of Mary's Conception	December 8
Nativity	December 25
Epiphany	January 6
Baptism	January 7
Candlemas	February 3
Ash Wednesday	February 11
Good Friday	March 27
Easter	March 29

The Sanctorale (Proper of Saints)

Winter

St. John the Apostle	December 27
St. Sebastian	January 20
Conversion of St. Paul	January 26
St. Timothy	January 26
St. Thomas Aquinas	January 28
Chair of St. Peter	February 22
Sts. Perpetua and Felicity	March 7
St. John of God	March 8
St. Catherine of Bologna	March 9
St. Joseph	March 19

Chapter 1

Carrots for the Stars

C ame they all to the little priory to behold the miracle. First
came the city men in red silks jangling with silver, then the
bishops in purple. Came they all yet turned away, for the miracle
was invisible but to the boy, and now the boy himself was invisible.

The men in red said the piece of plaster bearing the feet was
the painter's. The men in purple said they were the Christ's feet.
The boy knew only that he had rescued them because none should
lack feet. The high men's different tellings might have bewildered
the boy, for he was only ten years.

Many oft said "he is only ten years yet strong," though none
knew his age true. Sister Virginia Maria told to him once, on the
Feast of Mary's Conception, she fathomed him five years, and this
the boy never forgot. Every December 8th added he another year,
a precise weight upon an imprecise scale.

When the sum reached ten, and Sister Virginia Maria was
dead, Brother Filippo commissioned the boy assist the Priory construction, the rebuilding of two of its three chapels. "You are only
ten years yet you are strong," Brother Filippo said, also undertaking the boy would sleep in the stables and be brought food for the
whole of the construction. The boy would have labored for naught

but the fellowship of achievement, and for the miracle that the suffering body oft buckles the mind against suffering.

The work was physical hard, in the small moments. The hardest was lifting rotten timbers from the mounds of rubble and dragging them to the drays. The boy's hands bled with the stigmata of splinters. When finally he noticed that the workmen wrapped their hands in rags when attended they the old beetled wood, the boy did likewise, yet the cloth snagged the splinters already there and made them bleed all the more. He could not remove the smallest of them, for his fingertips were indelicate, worn by the labors.

The flats of plaster and lath, often larger than he, were lighter than the timbers yet so dusty just an hour of moving them sheltered him top to toes with white powder. Even the brows of his forehead and the lashes of his eyes caught and held the powder. A day moving plaster and lath left the boy unexhausted yet looking as the dead on the carts, dried of life and marked by the bleached ash. Yet unlike they the boy's eyes and lips burned through the white dust. Unlike they the boy could wash the dust clean at the well.

Near every third day, a hundred jagged stones the boy carried one by one, each oft heavier than he, making a hundred voyages to one pile on one day, only to take the same stones to another pile in another hundred voyages later. The boy did not object to these movings of stones. Their sharp edges often cut his hands, yet sometimes their blades also shaved the splinters gone.

When the small moments allowed of knitting together, at night ere sleeping or during the short break at Sext for drink, or even during the work when his mind small-stepped away, the boy frequent filled with pride. He had heard the workmen say this reconstruction was ordered by the King of Spain himself, and in those knitted moments the boy dreamed the King of Spain visiting the restored chapels, turning to commend the strong boy of ten for his keystone part, and handing him three gold coins.

Although they were brothers in the labors, little attention did the workmen pay the boy. They had not even recognized him when first he arrived to effort with them, though just the day past he was among the infestation of waifs poured daily through the

Priory walls opened by the construction. The waifs begged and stole jiffs of rags which wrapped they round their bony bodies. They begged and stole cooking tools which sucked they dry then scraped with their front teeth. Hid they in their tatters stolen peat for later warming.

But in the main they merely clouded round the constellation of construction fires, stealing warmth and making nuisance, smelly little moths attracted by the flames but fearing capture. Had the workmen paid the boy anywise attention, they would have witnessed him glance knowing to the swarm, passing them bits of rags and crumbs of food.

The boy began the day of his commission strange, accompanied by the chief foreman, who announced to the audience of workmen the boy would henceforth live in the stables and work the construction for his keep. These odd announcings stirred currents of wondering in the workmen, yet they soon fell to ignore the boy, save once early on, when the moth spoke of his pride for the building, of his dream about the King of Spain and the three coins of gold.

Upon this boasting, one of the workmen struck the boy so firm the prideful gnat dropped the timber he was dragging, which rolled and struck another workman. The man who struck him and the man whom the timber struck then beat the boy roundly. He was saved only when the chief foreman intervened, thrashing both men with his rod. "I will expel you from this construction, or worse, if this boy you ever touch again." All the workmen whispered anew of the boy's mysterious protections, yet quick returned the boy to anonymity.

As all the moths, the boy's memories from the convent orphanage were dim, the few sharp ones noisy and hard, a handful of clear lines separating one empty space from another. Sounds of gaggling nuns and ringing bells mixed with the prick of unhewn wood against sleeping spine, all floating in a pool of the food that was really just drink. They said Sister Virginia Maria acted as a mother to him, yet the boy could not verify, for he never knew what mothers did. He saw that Sister Virginia Maria wept more than the others when the Mother Superior ordered him leave, with a rucksack laid with food, drink, and blankets, the customary gift to all the older boys required to depart to make room for the babes. Perhaps this is what mothers mainly do, he thought, weep more than others.

All the sisters were kind to him, kinder than most of the brothers and certain kinder than the friars or the Prior. Yet it was the Prior who must have directed Brother Filippo commission the boy for the construction, who allowed the boy sleep in the stables, and who sent his servant feed the boy twice daily and clothe him anew when winter approached. To the boy, the Prior was near God, vanished by distance yet everywhere protecting. The workmen laughed at the boy's awe, and said things as, "A Dominican prior? Ha! He is no more a general of this army than you, lad. Now, a Benedictine abbot, there is a general!"

Like God, the friars were kind to the boy by their remote actions but unkind in daily life. They scowled and squirmed whenever coming upon him, faces twisted as from a foul odor. They would not speak to the boy, even if, especially if, he tried speak to them, which he rarely then never did. The boy thought their distant kindness all the more miraculous for their proximate revulsion, and thanked God for the mystery.

Brother Filippo was opposite the Prior and friars in this regard. In no position to move large levers of protection, Brother Filippo was content moving only small ones, always with a kind countenance lashed with gentle words. "How goes the construction?" he would ask, as if the boy were its architect or a foreman. "Is there aught I can help you with?" as if Brother Filippo were the Prior or the King of Spain. "Thanks be you for the commission, Brother Filippo," the boy would respond, which would lighten Brother Filippo's load, as if it had been his commission to give.

Brother Filippo saw the boy frequent, for Filippo was a blacksmith ere he found God and was thusly charged care of all the construction workhorses. He labored at the stables every day early, ere Prime, whether any true labor there be, and always brought the boy a handful of rags and a piece of peat, or sometimes even firewood. The stables were cold despight the smoke leaking under the locked door to the kitchen, despight the horses' warm bodies and hot breath, and despight the small fireplace. The smoke and horses warmed slight, yet far insufficient to the winter cold streaming tween the rafters.

The fireplace, cut into the east wall opposite the horses at the west, never roared but only squeaked, irregardless the bounty of fuel. Brother Filippo said its flue might need cleaning and undertook he would instruct the boy in the matter in the spring. In the meanwhile, Brother Filippo's gifts of warmth kept the boy alive in the coldest of the winter, and allowed him sleep through the night when spring began to show.

From Brother Filippo's eyes, the poor boy lived a life of sorrowful deprivation, as all the moths did, lives he was warm to improve in the small ways he could, with his small levers. Yet from the boy's eyes he was now warmer and safer than ever he could remember, except for the dim times at the orphanage, and thus a few scraps of wood and wool and bread found their way from the boy to the moths.

One special cold night, a flight of them landed at the stable doors begging entrance. The boy certain admitted them, to share the warmth of the horses, though the fire was long dead and no firewood or peat remained. One of the younger boys was pale with death, and all knew it would come soon whether he ate or not, whether he warmed or not. Yet also they knew food and warmth might comfort him until the end. So they placed him in the warmth betwixt the sleeping horses, who first startled at the intrusion yet quick composed. Then they covered him with straw and collected their bits of food and placed them on a pannikin before him. Yet he did not warm and did not eat. He died ere Lauds. The horses knew, and alerted the boys, who carried the dead child away fore the brothers began stirring.

The day next, Brother Filippo cautioned to the boy no outsiders were permitted on the Priory grounds least inside its buildings, even the stables, even the boy's friends, even his dying friends. The Brother warned that if outsiders were ever again found trespassed the Prior would banish Brother Filippo. Brother Filippo said these words with the hard wet eyes the boy saw regular in the brothers, and sometimes even in the friars, when they carried suffering news. The suffering carved deep gorges, and the tears carved them deeper still, suffering upon suffering.

The boy knew not how came Brother Filippo to the knowledge of his visitors, and inquired not. Yet the boy protested that the announced punishment would be unjust, that it should be he, the boy, who were banished, not Brother Filippo, if again the moths guested. Brother Filippo smiled and said this was the Prior's decision and it would not change. The boy told the moths, told to them they must die cold as they had always done, otherwise Brother Filippo, whom they loved for his charity, would be banished, and each of the moths understood and abided.

The cold was the demon only of the night, for daily work kept all warm, no matter how bitter frozen nor how distant the grey sun nor deep the snow. It called terrible at Vespers, as temperatures fell and working muscles tried rest, yet rest eluded for the shiverings kept them busy all night. And when sun rose and chased the one fiend, its cousin hunger took its place.

Hunger was the demon of the day. Brother Bartolomeo, the Prior's personal servant, a bent old man, brought the boy his meals, one shortly ere Prime then another tween Vespers and Compline. It was more food than the boy could remember ever placed before him, yet still it did not chase the hunger, for the hard work burned the food away like candlewax. Still, the boy saved small bits for the moths.

Brother Filippo never brought the boy food, yet the boy understood and forgave. Brother Filippo was a cathedral of a man, perhaps twenty-five stone. He would be as hungry as the boy with twice the food. He did little work that the boy witnessed, only an occasional shooing of the horses and tinkering with horsely fittings, and even these accomplished sitting on a stool. Yet just moving his twenty-five stone through the world was the daily labor of three men. When once the boy offered Brother Filippo a few scraps of dried rabbit, the giant man's face turned red, his eyes lowered, and he politely declined. The boy was sorrowful he had shamed the man, and silently vowed never again offer him food.

Work suspended Christmas Eve, Christmas Day, and the next. The boy would to have labored through these holy times, for he discovered early in his moth days too much rest tween hard strainings lulled the muscles lazy, and made the next laborings harder still. And yea it was that when returned they to the construction on St. John the Apostle's Day the work was twice hard for the boy and saw he also for all the workmen. Two full days it was until the lazy muscles woke full.

Three days past Epiphany, long past his evening meal, when he should have been sated and sleepy, the wax of his hunger candle burned special low, and the boy came seized of the smokeless kitchen smells still coming from under the locked door. He fought mighty to ignore the engines of temptation and then anew to resist them, yet both battles were fast lost. He ran to the door as a lunatic, pounded on it, scratched at it, then fell to his knees sobbing. The door was not special thick, yet it was newer than the rest of the stables, oak not pine, and stronger than a strong boy of ten years weakened by starvation.

Then the boy remembered the small piece of metal, thin and twisted and bight in half with slight crossing ends. He found it early in his commission and made it his own, with the foreman's permission. The rusty metal might have been a piece of a pig snare or part of a small dray's tongue assembly. It was corroded brown like all the other metal, but he scraped it clean with his small knife, and it almost shined.

From the pouch of his torn breeches the boy retrieved the tool, and tried slip one of its ends into the door's keyhole, though it proved too thick. Yet the other end fit as if it were the key itself. The boy readied joust with the clockworks inside, yet at his first effort the metal turned easy and the bolt asided.

The cooks were gone yet the embers of their fires till glowed, enough to illuminate dim the gems nearest. The boy had never been in the kitchen, never gazed upon what now he saw. Bags of wheat flour, barley, and millet stood as ten pins. Two tall racks of bread stood next, some loaves baked and some to be baked. Wooden crates of cabbages, turnips, garlic, onions, carrots, and potatoes, stacked high. Smelled he sharp vinegars and soothing oils, yet the dimness blinded him of their sources.

At the far end, furthest from the embers, the boy came upon a small unlocked door to a slat-walled room, small spaces tween the slats open to the cold outside. Skitterings of rats greeted him then quieted gone. The room was full with hanging rabbits, chickens, and sides of butchered lamb, all lit in stripes of moonlight. Under a blanket on a wooden shelf lay two eyeless pigs and next a bowl of eggs. The boy seized two eggs, replaced the blanket, then repaired from the moon-striped room. Seized he thirteen carrots from the kitchen crates, then locked the door behind with the magic key.

To each of his stable mates the boy fed one carrot. He had named the horses after the splashes of stars taught him by Sister Virginia Maria, for he had not known enough people in his short life to know twelve names different from the names of the friars, brothers, and sisters, and did not wish their holy names for the beasts. The orphans had names, but they, too, were holy names. The moths adopted names rough and sometimes offensive, also unfitting for the horses.

On clear nights Sister Virginia Maria showed to the boy the patterns of the stars and told to him the names of the patterns. She conducted the lessons in secrecy from the Mother Superior, and once whispered the boy that the Mother Superior was nay friend of the stars and that he should nary speak of the starly lessons to her. The boy memorized all the names, though he could never see the patterns Sister Virginia Maria saw.

Orion, Ursa Major, Ursa Minor, Canis Major, Canis Minor, Aquila, Cancer, Centaurus, Aquarius, Pleiades, Cassiopeia, and Pisces, each ate a stolen carrot and gave thanks to the boy. Even the nameless mule seemed thankful of its carrot.

Then cracked the boy the two stolen eggs, placed them on his pannikin, and held it over the low fire, switching it quick betwixt his rag-wrapped hands to avoid scald. It was good that the stable fireplace was on the wall behind the aligned stars, for they could smell the cooking eggs but could not organize to turn round to meet them. They jostled with desire then with hope then with resignation. The smell of the cooking eggs was too powerful for the boy to wait, and he slid them down his gullet whilst still they were runny and only mild warm. He sipped ice-sharded water from his pouch, then lay back on his straw, contented.

Then he saw them, possibly for the first time yet he could not be sure. Perhaps erstwhile he had looked but not seen. Yet now he saw. Faint images peeling off the north wall high, the wall of the kitchen door. He could not make them out, but could see a few faded men, heads turned in different ways. He fell to sleep and dreamed of eggs and carrots and of the men.

When woke, he was sure the men had only been in his dreams. Yet when looked he anew at the wall still they were there, even more of them now, scowling at the sin of his thefts. He could see them best in the darkness of Matins, hours ere the winter sun rose. He could not see the horses or the kitchen door or even the dead fireplace just paces from where he lay, for the stables were windowless and not allowing of much moonlight, yet he could see the reproachful men.

Chapter 2

Aquila

In the second night of scowling, by more men still and clearer, the boy took the magic key and discarded it onto the old pile of debris towering over the peat mounds, the moon lighting his way across the cloister, and prayed God forgiveness. At Prime he requested Brother Filippo hear his confession, yet Brother Filippo said it was not permitted, that only the friars could hear confessions. (To the friars' disapproval, the Prior early in his rule declared each of the Priory's handful of servants should be heretofore called "Brothers," though they be not ordained nor some even reverent, to make plain the singularity of their community. "Nay," complained the friars, "the words friar and brother are selfsame." "Exactly," replied the Prior, and he bought each of the newly named Brothers monkly brown cowls to reinforce their churchly belonging.)

At the Sext break for drink, Brother Bartolomeo appeared and summoned the boy to the Prior. The workmen buzzed with guessings as Brother Bartolomeo led the boy into the Priory, a palace into which the boy had not heretofore ventured. Its floors were so smooth the boy worried he might slip, its air so warm he worried his lungs might explode with joy, and its walls so adorned with painted images of bearded men he worried they might point their cragged fingers at him in accusation. The craftly carved frames of the paintings reminded the boy of his sinful twisted metal key, and he was thankful he had discarded it.

Brother Bartolomeo pounded on a wide oak door spanning the great height of the hall, then against it leaned his crooked body, and the door creaked open. When the widening space was wide enough, the boy saw God. He was wearing only the friars' simple white tunic, without the black hooded capuce. This was God, not just a nearling, for nay earthly Dominican would receive visitors, even a boy of only ten years, without his black capuce. The boy had never in his life seen a friar less his capuce. God also wore on the fourth finger of His right hand a ring holding a great bloody stone, and such ring no earthly friar would wear.

When saw he the capuce hanging on a stand behind God's wooden desk, the boy was doubly unsurprised, for God had no need of cloaks even in the bitterest of cold. The room's great snapping fire was for the pleasure only of God's earthly guests.

"Thank you, Brother Bartolomeo, you may leave us," God said in a deep and rich voice that did not surprise the boy. "Young man, we have nary formal met. I am Friar Alessandro, the Prior here. I understand from Brother Filippo that you would to make confession. I will hear it." God then donned an ordinary confessional stole.

The boy was surprised, but could not think why so God himself could not hear confessions, being, after all, He had given this power to His priests and could choose instead to retain it. Yet the boy did wonder why so God needed to hear the words, when surely He knew everything about the boy's sin.

"Father forgive me, for I have sinned," the boy recalled the incantations of introduction. "My last confession was more two years agone, on my last day at the convent orphanage. Yesterday night, I stole two eggs and thirteen carrots from the Priory kitchen."

"Thirteen carrots!"

"For the horses, my Lord, the twelve workhorses with whom I sleep."

"And you consumed the thirteenth?"

"Nay, my Lord, the thirteenth was for the poor mule."

"Why so did you steal this food?"

"Because I was hungry, my Lord. The work makes me so hard hungry, and the horses and mule work, too, and they are ribly thin. I know it was a great selfishness of me, except for the carrots."

"Fifteen Our Fathers."

The boy was never again hungry, not in the way he was former. Brother Bartolomeo brought him large meals of bread and milk and meat, feasts to the crumbs bygone. And with each feast came always a bowl of hot broth. This broth was not a meal disguised, as in the orphanage, but a hot warming feast of drink following upon a real feast of food. The boy had so much food he could now share generous with the moths, though he never offered any food to Brother Filippo. Every night, Brother Bartolomeo also brought a bowl of thirteen carrots.

Yet the men on the wall kept their scowling. The boy had done his penance, said his fifteen Our Fathers, yet each night the men stared down their displeasure. The more the boy looked at them the more he could see the colors and shapes that had flaked off so long ago. The boy asked Brother Filippo about the fresco, but Brother Filippo knew nothing of it. He had not even noticed the dissolved images and flaking plaster until the boy asked of them.

Each night the fresco grew clearer and more vigorous to the boy, even as the squeaking fire went weak and cold and the stables darkened to near black. Soon the fresco's health spread across the entirety of the wall, each night displacing more flakings and faint remainings. Perhaps these men are not scowling at my sins, the boy thought, perhaps they are scowling at another's, or at one another's. On the fourth night, the boy began to see the table, and realized the scowling men were eating whilst they scowled.

On the sixth night, the fresco was complete, and the boy wept. He wept first at the fresco, at its meaning, though he could not have told the meaning. He wept next for the fresco, at the scar the kitchen door had inflicted on it, removing the feet of the tall man sitting in the center of the table, though he could not have told why the desecration so moved him.

The day following, when Brother Bartolomeo brought the morning meal, the boy asked him of the fresco. Brother Bartolomeo said he knew naught of it, save that it was done long ago. He said he did not know what the fresco once showed, for it was now so damaged it showed nothing. The boy did not tell that the fresco had become clear to him. He asked Brother Bartolomeo if the Prior might know of the fresco, and Brother Bartolomeo said he was unsure.

Two days further, serving the evening meal, Brother Bartolomeo said that the Prior would visit the boy after Compline. The boy did not know what to do of this visit from God. The stables reeked of smoke from the wood fires in the kitchen and from the boy's peat fires and stank hard from the stars' leavings. Every morning ere beginning his commission the boy propped open the stable doors so that the towering smells might leave, yet a sapling of them always remained, now joined by the cold. Every morning and evening the boy cleaned the stables and placed the manure in a barrel outside, yet his stars seemed always to exceed his efforts, especially now with the feasts of carrots. But surely God would not be offended at fires smoking or horses shitting, for He had designed them both. Still, the boy was worried about this visit, so worried he neglected to plan what he would say to God about the feasting and angry men on the north wall.

"Good evening, my young man. I understand you have questions about this fresco," and God pointed to the wrong wall, to the south wall and its beautiful images of the crucifixion, walking toward it with his candle.

"Nay, my Lord, that one," and the boy pointed to the north wall.

"I see nay fresco on that wall," and God drew closer, bringing his candle. "Ah, yes, this is an old fresco so badly done it was lost long ago, ere I and a score of my predecessors came to this Priory. You can see here the dim-colored plaster has peeled off and is still peeling," and the Prior lifted his candle toward the perfectly rendered wide brown sandals of the man in the bright blue tunic and green cape standing at the left side of the table.

The boy thought to himself, *Yet if you look at it longly, my Lord, as I have done, you can make out everything. Men in bright costumes at table, talking and scowling. I thought previous they were scowling at me. But every night the fresco became clearer, with no need of candles. As the images cleared the message dimmed, and now I am unsure why so the men scowl.* But the boy did not say these words. God could not see the men or the table. To Him, the fresco was just crumbs, an eye here, part of a hand there, falsely connected by a boy's imagination. Yet He seemed uncommon interested in the imagination.

He told the boy the stables once were the friars' refectory, and that one of His predecessors cut the hole for the door to give traverse to the kitchen, so that the poor cooks need no longer walk out and round to the refectory's door when they served the priests their meals. He said He had heard that both frescos were made at the same time, but did not know why so the one on the south wall survived whilst the one on the north did not. The boy did not tell to Him that the fresco on the north wall had survived.

The boy forgave the Prior's predecessor for ordering the door cut in the middle of the fresco, surmising that, like the Prior, his predecessor was to the fresco blind. The boy wondered why so, if he could clearly see a fresco long ago dissolved, he could not also see what had been in the space where the door had been cut. This miracle seemed jagged to the boy, and not at all Godly.

For many days the boy forgot about the God who could not see and the space that could not be imagined. Each day, the weather seemed to grow a trifling less cold and Vespers to come a trifling later. The boy's stars were livelier, at work and at night, although that might have been owing to the carrots.

Every night, after the boy fed the carrots to his stars and to the little mule, took his meal, and stoked the fire if there was fuel, he lay down to stare at the men on the wall. They now looked more worried than angry. Afore, he fathomed them fighting over the food. Yet now he could see loaves of bread and cuts of eel garnished with oranges. Perhaps the men were heavy discussing how much of the food to parcel to the poor. The boy also now saw the small groups of men whispering, and wondered about the workmen whispering.

The boy was able to keep these great wonderings out of his thinkings during the day, to store them in the stables as the brothers stored roots in the cellar. This storing of the great nightly wonderings permitted the boy to see all the smaller wonderings of his work day. The cold water at Sext, plated with ice, quenched a thirst that was somehow hot despight the frigid air. The timbers did not always stab him, and even when they did they oft seemed repentant. Occasionally, a marriage of plaster and lath was peaceful and orderly, and mysteriously not clouded dusty. Some of the stones were smoothed of their cutting edges and thusly made lighter. And when the work and these small wonderings were done, the boy returned to the stables and retrieved the great wonderings.

On the Feast of the Conversion of Saint Paul, as the boy was moving a pile of stones from a place east of the stables to a place west, he heard commotion in the cloister, lashed screams of man and horse. The boy ran toward the noises and saw a workman beating Aquila, the newest of the stars, joined even after the boy joined. The workman was admonishing the horse move, to pull a dray heavy with the boy's timbers, but the great roan gelding would not move. When the boy first saw them, the man was beating Aquila with a heavy broad crop, first on withers then on flanks. Aquila's broad brown sides hatched red with dripped crossings of blood and his eyes bulged with fear, yet still he would not move.

Then the man abandoned the crop and lifted a heavy stone. With both hands heaved he the stone over his head and down onto Aquila's back right hoof. The horse screamed, and began to rear but the damaged hoof could not bear the rearing. Still, Aquila would not forward move.

The boy pleaded the man stop yet the man ignored, lifting another stone larger than the last. The boy retrieved the discarded crop and began beat the man with it. Confused, the man turned to face the boy, then snarled and raised the stone toward the boy.

Aquila kicked the man dead with one blow, the man's brained open forehead stamped with the bloody mark of the horse's raw hoof.

The foreman and chief foreman in turn inquired of the boy what occurred, for no soul witnessed the event save the boy, the man, and Aquila. The boy told true, yet was unsurprised Brother Bartolomeo again summoned him to the Prior. This time, the Prior was wearing his black capuce over his white tunic, though the hood was down round his shoulders. He was smiling, but the boy saw confusion in the smile.

"I would not to discuss with you the incident today at the west cloister wall. A man died, but it was by his own cruel hand, not by your hand nor the hooves of the innocent beast, for whom I will pray St. Eligius. It was poor of you striking the man, but it was not a sin." The Prior bid the boy sit upon a chair opposite the fire, and the boy obeyed. "I would instead to discuss the painting on the north wall of the stables. I have conducted some research into our texts, and have become learned in some aspects."

The Prior told the boy the two frescos had each been commissioned by Duke Francesco himself, ere the French and then Spanish took the city. The Duke's son remodeled many parts of the Priory, intending its church become his family's mausoleum. The crucifixion fresco on the south wall was completed by a local artist, the son of famous painters who toiled for decades in the city's cathedral.

The fresco on the north wall was not fresco at all. It was painted by Leonardo himself, a name known even to the boy. It was the original of The Last Supper, everywhere now copied, a painting's name the boy also knew, though he had never seen a copy. The Prior told the boy the master put the paint direct on the surface of the dry plaster instead of mixing the color into wet plaster. This is why so the painting flaked off when the dry plaster flaked off. "This is what I know. But tell me what you know. What you see."

The boy described the entire painting to the Prior, the beautiful colors of the men's tunics and cloaks, their smooth faces, their confusing countenances, the shadowed edges with no lines, the faces holding emotions, the bountiful food and drink. He told of the men whispering, some angry, some in disbelief, and one holding a knife. The boy told of how the painting had made him cry when it revealed, and that still he did not know why so he cried. The boy told of how the missing feet of the man in the middle of the table, the feet stolen by the kitchen door, also made him cry, and that, again, he did not know why so. The boy told of how he could best see the fresco at night, without aid of candle or moon.

The Prior asked the boy how old he was, and the boy told him he was of ten years, yet strong. The Prior laughed, genuine and happy, and asked whether the stables were warm enough and would the boy to move into the Priory. The boy replied nay, that he could never leave the stars behind, explaining the stars as the horses, and the Prior smiled.

Brother Filippo treated poor Aquila's lashes with a warm poultice he made with bread, flax, and mustard, and tried repair the gelding's crushed hoof with a series of wraps soaked in the same poultice and supported by a contraption of wooden rods lashed to the horse's leg with strips of leather. Aquila could not pull the drays with just three good legs, and thusly remained in the stables near a week whilst the other stars worked.

Aquila submitted trusting to Brother Filippo's ministrations, for the gelding loved the large man, who was always gentle in his horsely applications. Yet Aquila's hoof did not improve. On the sixth day of missed work, the chief foreman told that if Aquila absented just two more days, they would have to kill him.

The boy had seen men kill workhorses, seen them smash their brains out with heavy hammers. Once, when the hammer blows failed, the boy saw workmen stab the convulsing horse dead. It took many thrusts and many minutes for the convulsions to stop and the horse's soul to rise. The boy prayed God save Aquila these fates, and his prayers were answered.

Aquila died in the night of the seventh day after his injuries. Brother Filippo, who demanded stay the nights in the stables to watch over his patient, was sleeping when the boy heard the stars begin singing a low song. The boy rose, and saw Aquila down and breathing hard, the other stars circling him, still singing. The singing stopped when the boy approached, and the stars made way of the circle for the boy to enter. Aquila stopped breathing soon after the boy lay down with him. Brother Filippo, awakened by the boy's sobs, tried comfort him, telling him that Aquila died from poison in his blood released by the blows to his hoof, yet the boy knew he had killed him with his prayers.

The foreman said they were in nay need of another horse, that they already had too many, and in the events the construction was nearing end. So the stars became eleven. In the light of the sun and the challenges of their labors, the eleven did not seem to grieve for Aquila nor even notice his absence. Yet every night, when Vespers came, the boy heard his stars sing their sad prayers.

Chapter 3

His Feet

When learned the boy from the Prior that the stables had been a refectory, and an opening made in its north side to communicate it with the kitchen, the boy remembered the faint images on the great piece of plaster he'd found weeks agone. He had just begun his commission, and the foreman instructed him carry a wooden box heavy of rusted metal to the tall pile of rubble near the peat mounds. The boy was to discard the metal and return the box.

The peat was piled autumn high but the rubble even higher. The boy threw each piece of rusted metal as far up the mountain as he could, not as a game, though it became one, but because the foreman had instructed him to do so, to prevent the mountain from spreading wide at its bottom and invading the territory of the peat. The only piece the boy did not discard was the thin twisted metal that would become the key to the kitchen door, the key to his sins of gluttony.

The last piece in the box was the lightest, a small broken brass hinge that had been forged as an eagle but was now just a flange and a half-wing. When the boy threw it, it flew and took a high and bighted path to the back side of the mountain, closer to the top than any of the boy's throws previous. When the eagle bit into the back of the mountaintop, it caused an avalanche, and when the years of castoffs finally rested and the white dust cleared, the boy saw at his feet a very large piece of jagged plastered wall.

It was propped against the base of the now much widened mountain, and the boy could see on it a handful of pale images. The boy was mild interested by the faint shapes, but could not delay, for when the mountain slid wide, now so close to the peat, he worried he would be thrashed by the foreman. He spent as much time as he could bear narrowing the mountain's girth, and he flung the piece of wall to the side with little thinkings.

Yet now the boy wondered whether the large plaster wall he had released then discarded had come from the north wall of the stables, from the opening to the kitchen, from the amputated painting. He was unsure. It did not seem sufficient large, as massive as it was, and he remembered no feet, just faint shapes. Still, the boy settled he would look for the piece of wall when first he could.

But this plan asundered with villainy: a fire set deliberate at the stables. The villain was the brother of the man Aquila killed. Workmen had overheard the man vow revenge on "that worthless bastard boy and his bags of bones," and reported same to the chief foreman. The chief foreman cautioned the man, but the man hid his wild revenge with the countenance of reason dragged with grief. On the night of Candlemas, tween Matins and Lauds, placed the man at the stable doors several large bales of hay garnished with peat and twigs, and lit the mixture afire. Brothers preparing for Lauds saw the flames and the shadow of the man, and rang the Priory awake. What happened next no one could certain say.

The flight of the boy, the horses, and the mule was blocked by the flames. Neither could they exit through the mighty kitchen door, for it was locked and the boy had discarded the sinful key. Yet the flames suddenly departed. Brothers found the burning mixture far from the stables, and the villainous man unconscious near the well. One of the brothers, Vincenzo, claimed he saw an old-style knight on a black steed push the burning mass from the stable doors with his lance, yet Vincenzo was well-known to drink generous in the blood of Christ, oft to the point of fancy. Another brother, Stefano, claimed he saw a musketeer strike the villain upon the head with the butt of his weapon and drag him to the well, yet Stefano was of famously poor sight.

The stars and the boy were startled by the flames, but when the threat was gone the boy walked them slow through the grounds to show them all was well, and they soon settled. The stupid little mule knew not of the danger, and returned to the stables even whilst the ground at the door still warmed.

The friars locked the villain in the root cellar until soldiers from the city retrieved him. The boy heard tales the man was hanged, and that the Prior attended the hanging and gave the man the Viaticum, but no one spoke of this. Yet all spoke of the boy's ethereal rescuers, the knight and the musketeer. Much of these discussings were laid to mock the drunk and blind witnesses, who maintained their testimony, yet much was not in jest but rather wedded to the other mysteries surrounding the boy.

It was the sounds of these wedded mysteries that the Mother Superior must have heard, when the wind and gossipers carried them miles into the mountains to the convent. She dispatched an orphan to message the Prior she would visit upon the morn. No Mother Superior from this convent nor any other had visited the Priory in living memory, and the Prior did not know the procedures governing such visit. It mattered not, for the Mother Superior's only request was to see the boy, the boy God had selected from the moths, the boy rescued from hellfire by dead knights and soldiers. The Prior thanked God word of the boy's paintly visions had not reached into the mountains.

The boy had not seen the Mother Superior since she was at the back of the retinue as the sisters bid the boy and his rucksack farewell. In his memory, she was a fierce and glaring hurricane, even more fierce and glaring than the men on the wall. Her fierceness grew when the boy learned from Sister Virginia Maria that the Mother Superior was no friend of the splash of stars in God's heavens. How could anyone be devout of His building without also being devout of the materials for its construction?

Yet when the Mother Superior entered the churchyard, the boy saw no storm, only an old woman becalmed from the long walk. She knocked at the Priory door and trickled in when Brother Bartolomeo opened it. After some time passed, Brother Bartolomeo summoned the boy.

It was all a trick. Mother Superior was pretending to be an old woman but the boy saw at once she was the same tempest he had known. The Prior introduced her politely, and the boy bowed, but she said nary a word. She grabbed his face and twisted his head this way and that, turning her own head that way and this as if in a mirror. She pulled the boy's jaw down with one of her hands, holding his forehead with her other, and looked in his mouth, as horsemen examine marketed mounts. She rolled up both legs of the boy's worn breeches, considered the limbs both front and back, and harrumphed. Then she waved the boy out of the room, as if she were the Prior. The boy looked to the Prior, who nodded his assent, and the boy left.

Immediately to the peat mounds the boy flew, to find the discarded wall panel. He could not remember exact where he had tossed it, and could not find it in the short time allowed, for he knew the foreman would be expecting him back at work. Perhaps, he mused, the Mother Superior's body investigations decreased his finding skills.

The rest of the boy's day was pleasant mixed tween timber dragging and stone hauling, an unusual blending, for mostly a day was dedicated solely to one task. When saw he the Mother Superior's gale blow across the grounds and out the gate, the boy expected to be summoned again to the Prior, but they never spoke of her visit.

The Prior did summon the boy the day following, but to discuss the business of the fire. "Two brothers claim they saw rescuers," he laughed, "but they were tired and the night was moonless. How think you the ball of fire found its way one hundred feet afar the stable entrance?"

The boy said he did not know.

"Do you still see the painting on the north wall clearly?" The boy said he did. He did not mention the images seemed to dim slightly after Aquilas's death, for he was sure this was his grieving imagination. "Do you see what was painted on the wall ere the door was installed?" The boy said he could not see what had been on the removed wall. He hesitated, but then told the Prior of the large piece of lathed plaster he found near the peat mounds, and that he thought it might be the piece of wall that had been removed for the door.

The Prior's words said that this was impossible, that it was too long ago, that a piece of lathed plaster outdoors would nary survive the years of snowy winters and wet springs, nor the swords of wind in autumn, but his eyes were less sure. He asked whether the markings on the piece of wall showed clear to the boy, and the boy said nay, that he saw only faint shapes, much as he saw the full painting afore it cleared. The Prior paused, looked at the grand clock on the mantle, and said, "You and I shall now endeavor find this missing piece of wall and return it home."

Never before had the boy seen the Prior in the open air. He assumed the great man might garden with the brothers and other friars in the summer months, yet the boy had never been inside the Priory walls in summer. He and the other moths could never enter the grounds until this season's chapel workings breached the walls. Occasionally, a moth or two managed to scale the parapets, but never the boy, for he was reluctant to intrude, even with the dogs of hunger at his heels. The boy was great skeptical when one of the trespassing moths spoke of rivers that ran with milk and cows that shat blocks of cheese and butter, and greater still when the tale teller would not assent to repeat his trespasses and return with the bounty.

Wore the Prior his thick black capuce, pulled tight against the cold, and a square black hat. Wore the boy his usual rags. All in the churchyard stared at them, until the Prior dismissed their looks with a flick of his rubied hand and all returned to their work, sneaking only occasional glances. The boy walked the Prior to the peat mounds, now considerable lower than in autumn, and showed him the ancient tower of refuse. The Prior held a thin white cloth over his nose, and complained with the shape of his face about the stench, but said naught. He put the white cloth away, and communicated his plan of search.

"We will begin search in an ever-widening circle, using this large mass of refuse as the navigating center of the circle. But first, we must certain the piece of wall is not in the large mass itself, that someone has not thrown it back upon it." He circled the tower. He lowered his head in thought. "It has only been two months past you discarded the wall near the bottom of this mass. If a workman had tossed it back, it cannot be deep. We should be able to see it if only we could get sufficient high." Then after a long pause, "Eureka!"

Man and boy returned apace to the Priory, this time the Prior ignoring all the watchful eyes. Summoned he the chief foreman and inquired how many times in the two months previous had any workmen placed new refuse on the large pile near the peat mounds. The foreman explained the large pile was from yore but now used only to discard glass and metal, which news seemed to please the Prior. The chief foreman then consulted some workbooks and reported that in the last two months only a small amount of such material had been removed from the construction sites and discarded on the old refuse pile, only three small wooden boxes full.

The chief foreman and his assistants grumbled considerable when the Prior years past directed them make detailed records of all materials coming to the Priory for the constructing and even of all disposings. Their grumblings grew special for the disposings, as never once had the Prior ever consulted them of the recorded disposings. And how so would anyone attend to disposing? Yet they obeyed, and now the chief foreman smiled at the request though he remained blind to its reasons.

Inquired then the Prior where broken plaster lathings disposed, and the chief foreman in answer reported they were burned weekly, more often if needed, in the main construction fire. Again, the Prior directed the chief foreman consult the disposing records, which made the chief foreman now doubly happy yet still without improvement to his blindness. The chief foreman reported that in the two months past just two drays of plastered lathings and wood were burned. He reported the days—the latest one a fortnight ago and the earlier three—yet upon further inquiry of the Prior admitted the records did not separately text wood from lathings. The Prior thanked and dismissed him.

The tower of refuse must still be scanned, the Prior told to the boy, for a lazy workman might well ignore the rules that only metal and glass be disposed there. The Prior walked quickly through the church to the campanile, the boy running behind. The two ran the stairs as hasty and excited as monkeys in trees. At pinnacle, and breathing heavy, opened the Prior the western window, so that their vision not be fogged by the dirty glass. Both Prior and boy gazed down at the top of the refuse pile, which from such great height appeared as a small bush, but neither man nor boy could see the piece of wall.

"Tell me again its dimensions, my son." The boy repeated the piece of wall was taller than he by half and wider by thrice, and boy and Prior again scoured the ground from their height, not just the bump of refuse but as well round it, performing with their eyes the plan of navigating search the Prior had told for their feet. Seeing naught, they descended.

The Prior told they would search again tomorrow, after Terce. When the boy responded he was needed for work, the Prior smiled and said he would arrange the matter with the chief foreman. When the Prior told they would mount horses for the search, the boy responded the horses, too, were needed for work. The Prior smiled once again, and said he would arrange that matter as well. "Select two horses, saddle them, and bring them to the Priory doors at Terce." When the boy explained there were no saddles for these workhorses, the Prior said they would ride on blankets.

The boy could not decide which of the eleven stars to take on this journey. For a few moments he worried about favoring any of them, but they sang comfort to him that all their spirits would be with him on the search. So he selected the smallest mare for himself, Cassiopeia, and the largest stallion for the Prior, Ursa Major. He selected two of the best blankets, each with only a few small holes from the beetle larvae, and shook the vermin from them as best he could. He placed the blankets on the two horses and led them from the stables, apologizing to the other stars, who forgave him and reminded their spirits were with him.

The Prior greeted the boy at the Priory door, holding two fine blankets thick with embroidery. The Prior threw the blankets over the horses, on top of the boy's blankets, and the explorers headed to the peat hills, again under the relentless and ignored stares of all in the yard. The Prior repeated his plan of searching in increasing wide navigations centered on the spire of waste, yet when arrived they at the peat hills Cassiopeia refused the boy's urgings and instead walked straightly south, beyond the last peat hill then beyond the well and the Priory gardens. The Prior commanded the boy return, and the boy turned his head and held out his hands to show that the little horse was walking in charge.

The Prior understood the signal, and trotted Ursa Major to meet them. The expedition winded its way slow through the south vineyard and the grove of olive trees. Cassiopeia did not stop until reached she the farthest corner of the Priory's walls, where the south and east walls conjoined, the very spot scaled not so long ago by the most courageous moths. There, leaning against each side of wall, perfectly in the meeting corner, was the piece of lathed plaster.

Man and boy dismounted and stared at it. The Prior asked the boy what he saw, and the boy described nothing more what the Prior saw: a few long shapes, some horizontal some vertical, with only hints of different greys. Yet the boy also told he was sure these were the tall man's feet. The two discussed the manner in which this piece of wall might have travelled to this remote corner, without resolution. The Prior explained he would to repeat the miracle of the stables by returning the plaster and lath there to see if its images grew in the boy's eye, as had done with the mother painting.

The Prior cursed Satan for making him forget the mule or extra horse to carry the piece of wall back to the Priory. The boy averred they could together ride on Ursa Major and strap the piece of wall to Cassiopeia, yet the Prior worried that without pack saddle the wall might fall and be lost. Instead, found they sturdy olive branches and built a small travois. Wrapped they the piece of wall in the two sets of blankets, secured with sinews of grape vines, and ever so slow, at half-walking speed, did Ursa Major and the Prior drag the piece of wall to the stables, Cassiopeia and the boy following on guard.

When the dragging team arrived home, the boy suggested they tack the piece of wall to the kitchen door to closely align it to its origins, yet again the Prior worried that the plaster would nary survive such attachment. Instead, they leaned it careful against the door, and the hunting party returned to daily work.

At the end of Nones, when all stars returned to the stables, they seemed quick happy at reuniting with their hunting friends, yet then resumed the nightly songs of mourning for Aquila. After Compline, the Prior visited the boy, anxious for his account. The boy reported that the painting was as clear as ever, not mentioning the imagined dulling, which persisted, but that the piece of wall leaning against the kitchen door remained as before. The Prior preached patience. After two more weeks, the situation remained. The Prior directed the workmen build a frame for the piece of wall and attach it and the frame delicate to the kitchen door, which they did, yet still naught changed.

On the Monday following the Feast of the Chair of Saint Peter, the chief foreman gathered the workmen in the churchyard and announced the construction work complete, save for few matters the foremen themselves and a handful of artisans would attend. He thanked the men, paid them, and sent them out to their new uncertainties. At least spring was soon, and there should be no more snow in these lower climes.

The Prior told to the boy all the horses would be sold at market, save one, and the boy was to select the one to keep as his own. Neither the boy nor the Prior wept, yet only because both willed themselves so. The boy selected Cassiopeia, as the Prior guessed he would. The Prior directed Brother Filippo lead the other horses to the paddock near the Priory gate, and to blanket them for the coming nights, to await their transport to the city later in the week. The Prior explained to the boy it would best if the separation were quick and firm. The boy understood, and thought of the day he left the crying sisters.

The Prior asked the boy again whether he would to move into the Priory, and the boy again declined. The Prior knew that this wound of the horses was fresh, and hoped the boy would agree to move when it was healed.

That night, Cassiopeia and the boy wept for hours. Even the mule, too small and stupid for weeping, sensed something crooked. Tween sobs they could hear the dirges of the stars from the paddock, louder than ever despight distance, for now they mourned both what had been and what was to be. Tween tears the boy looked up to the men on the wall, looked to them for wisdom. Perhaps their faces would tell him how to grieve the coming loss. But the faces were cloudy and indistinct. Sure that it was his tears blurring them, the boy wiped his eyes dry. Still the men were faint. They had faded away, almost to where they had been at the beginning. The boy fell to sleep in an agony of loneliness. He had lost his stars and now he had even lost his wise men on the wall.

He was awakened suddenly, long ere Lauds, by the cold. Poor little Cassiopeia and the even littler mule made such slight heat. They were to the roaring stars as the small stable fireplace was to the Prior's wide hearth. The boy awoke shivering, yet also shivered with an idea. He jumped to feet and to the paddock ran swift. The stars were happy to see him. The boy gave them their carrots that Brother Bartolomeo had without thinking continued to deliver to the stables with the boy's evening meal, carrots which in his misery that night the boy forgot to feed. The boy told the stars what he had discovered, what they already knew, and he comforted them.

Then he ran to the Priory, through its unlocked entrance, and pounded on the Prior's study door. Poor Brother Bartolomeo came out from behind a smaller nearby door and cursed at the boy for the intrusion. But the old man saw the truth in the boy's eyes and grumbled down the hall to another small door, upon which he knocked. The Prior emerged also grumbling but he, too, saw the truth in the boy's eyes.

"Tell me what you know, boy."

Chapter 4

The Stars and the Men

T he boy told of the men on the wall dissolving when the
stars left to paddock, that it was the stars who kept the wall
men clear and healthy. The boy did not tell of the slight dimming
when Aquila died, for still he believed this imagination. The Prior
firstly thought the boy's claims tying horse to paint a clever lie,
said by the boy desperate to save his beloved stars. But when to
the boy he proposed this explanation, the truth in the boy's eyes
grew yet stronger.

The Prior, the boy, and Brother Bartolomeo, he still grumbling, walked the stars back to the stables, each leading but a
single horse. As each triplet arrived, the constellations shuffled in
increased happiness. When finally the boy returned Ursa Major,
the Prior asked the boy if the faces had returned. The boy told the
Prior patience was required, and the Prior smiled.

The faces did not return that night, and the stars continued
their regular dirges for their lost Aquila. The boy wondered how
long this would continue, and then wondered more general about
grief. He could still feel his grief for Aquila, sharp and uninvited
as bygone. The boy believed the grief would change in the manner of its calling, as did the grief for his dead moths. That grief

never left yet he felt it only when he thought it, rather than the feelings trespassing the thoughts, as the grief for Aquila trespassed. He wondered whether the stars achieved a different peace because they did not think. He envied the stupid mule, which did not even know Aquila gone least grieve the going.

The boy asked of Brother Filippo how long lasted the cuts of loss ere healing in the soul. Brother Filippo told the boy a story of a mourning couple in the town where ere he toiled as a blacksmith.

"In this town lived an honest tradesman, a mason, and his wife. The two had been espoused more a year, but could nary conceive. They prayed nightly St. Anne, but still the wife grew nay child. Their priest advised them pray St. Anne hourly, and to follow the prayers with Hail Marys, one at Lauds, two at Prime, and so on until eight prayers at Matins of the next day, thirty-six Hail Marys all told. The wife jested that this answer would never tell, for it left them no time to lay with one another, but the man did not laugh and the two followed the priest's prescriptions. Still, no child grew.

"In the third year, desperate, the wife prayed the old gods of the land, who turned seed into wheat and dead vines into grapes, and shortly after these pagan prayers she was with child. The boy was born and grew fast and tall like the poplars. But in his seventh year, the child took ill and died. The old gods who pushed him up out of the soil took him back, for poplars die in their time, and they told the woman so. She replied, 'But the boy not a poplar he, and should have lived to three score.' The pagan gods, angry at the ungrateful woman, planted in her soul the seeds of grief, but these, too, lasted only seven years, for the seeds of life and of grief are selfsame."

The boy was surprised when the story ended thusly, and Brother Filippo could see the boy's surprise. So he explained that in His wisdom God weaved the vestments of grief to match in length the vestments of happiness, and that this was why so the wife had to grieve for seven years, for her sorrow to match her joy. When the boy told Brother Filippo that the grief he felt for Aquila was already longer in days than the days he had known the horse, Brother Filippo could not explain. "Perhaps," he said, "the grief must match the days of the horse, whether you knew the horse or not."

The boy knew not how long Aquila had lived, so inquired he of Brother Filippo, who said he was nay expert in fixing the ages of horses exact. But the general rule might inform, so the boy then inquired of the blacksmith how long horses live in the main. Brother Filippo knew of horses that lived for 30 years, yet he was too kind to tell the boy so. Instead, he comforted him, saying, "Only a few years, and by my looks Aquila was an old oak, with probably yet a few months to live." The boy was only ten years, yet he was no babe. He knew horses lived considerable more than few years, and he silent thanked Brother Filippo for his kindly lies but still ached to know the length of grief's candle.

The men on the wall began their return the next night, and the boy joyously reported the return to the Prior, who at once cancelled the horses' consignment with the market, even paying a small penalty. When the boy reported on the fourth night that the painting was as clear as former (less the untold dimming when Aquila died), the Prior praised God and began to think of politics. This could be a miracle, and a miracle would mean bishops and archbishops and, God forbid, officious meddling from Rome itself. This process has already begun, thought he, with the interferings of the Mother Superior.

The Prior had known all along of the boy's provenance, knowledge that the scold from the mountains might just ere have guessed. Yet the boy's provenance alone, even bound with knowledge why the Prior had selected him from the moths and why his life had been saved by mysterious warriors, would not land the boy on the shores of miracle. Least as long as the old nun did not discover the mystery of the horses and the men on the wall. This mystery had at all costs to be sealed secret, until God showed the way.

With the construction all but finished, the boy's work changed sharp, and now felt he currents of guilt for eating the Prior's food and sleeping in his stables. His construction tasks now were small, with occasional laborings inside the two chapels, removing spent materials and cleaning. Yet in the main, the boy's workday revolved around the stars, for they also stopped most of their work and for that selfsame reason needed they exercise. So the boy spent half of each day exercising them, riding them, one star at a time, round the inside circumference of the Priory walls. He exercised them in the same order every day, and they knew who was to be next, and each became excited at its turn.

The boy knew naught of miles, but he knew from his moth days that the city was but an hour's easy walk and the convent orphanage a hard four. By his fathoming of the speeds of walking and trotting, conservatively ignoring he sometimes galloped the stars, the boy summed he rode the stars to the city and back every day, and to the convent orphanage and back in a week's time.

He began to imagine actual riding the stars to these places. He and Ursa Major would be cheered by the city's nobles for their signal constructings, then honored with a special feast. They would feed Ursa Major fresh apples and the boy a roasted chicken, and place a garland of flowers across the star's great chest. At the convent, the sisters would surround the boy and Cassiopeia twittering and gushing at the boy's success, though the Mother Superior would stand off and her thunder rumble. The sisters' love would be the peace that stopped the boy's grieving. Alas, these were dreams, and the boy was not feted nor his grief abated.

Although his daily times in the chapels were short, the boy's soul soared there, pulled by the frescoes on the arched ceilings. The rounded scenes matched perfectly the curving calls to heaven. He had never seen such colors and shapes, such complications of man, animal, and God, save on the fresco of the crucifixion opposite the wall of men, and on which, because of the men calling him always north, he so seldom glanced, and which in the event was flat and did not bight him to heaven as these chapel curvings did.

The sisters made all the eldest orphans memorize many of the stories of the holy book, but did not tell the meanings of the stories. When asked the boy of Sister Virginia Maria about this lack, she explained the meanings must be discovered, as seeing the moment of an interesting cloud, and could not be told from one to another as passing a jug of water. But without the meanings, the stories floated untethered to the boy's memories. He could not identify a single story from the miracles of the chapel frescoes.

He oft thought of measuring these floating songs of color, in both chapels and in the crucifixion fresco, to the painting on the north wall of the stables, but the two could not be measured to the one. The chapel and crucifixion frescoes were glorious songs of men dressed as gods, whilst the painting on the wall was a mystery of gods dressed as men. The images themselves were incomparable. The flying faces of the chapel and thick faces of the crucifixion were beautiful surfaces, sharply lined edges defining their beauty. The faces on the wall had unlined edges, and their shadowed surfaces whispered of hidden interiors silent in the others.

One day, the boy approached one of the few chapel painters still finishing the floating surfaces, to ask him of these differences, but the foreman in charge ordered the boy away ere he could pose his questions.

The boy also began to think frequent of the puzzle presented by his new commissions, and why so he took vast more pleasure tending to the stars than gazing at the flying images in the chapels. The chapel frescoes vaulted his soul up and out to God's campanile where all could be seen. Still, the flying frescoes, even the one in the Chapel of the Holy Crown showing the men with spears, the one they said was painted by the famous Venetian, did not stir him as his stars stirred him. The stars were alive, and the paintings in the chapel only stories of life. And the painting on the north wall was something greater still.

Despight Brother Filippo's promise of approaching relief, the boy remained hobbled by grief for Aquila. He saw the dead star everywhere, in the castings of the straw, in the flames from firewood, in peat smoke, in the clouds. Each of his stars would sometimes take Aquila's form, trotting as he had trotted, galloping as the boy imagined Aquila would have galloped, even dying in the boy's dreams as Aquila died.

The boy also remained troubled by the faint images on the wall now secured on the kitchen door. This missing piece of the painting has finally after years been reunited with its mother, and the mother speaks yet the child holds mute. If only the stars could talk, thought the boy, they would teach me the secret of this mystery. After all, had not Cassiopeia found the missing piece of wall? The Prior regularly visited the boy, regularly disappointed both by the boy's continuing reports on the mute kitchen door and by his continuing declinations of the Prior's invitations to relocate to the warmer Priory.

Five full weeks afore the Feast of Saints Perpetua and Felicity, Brother Filippo woke the boy early and explained his plans. They would take food and clothing to the moths, and Brother Filippo would early preach them the story of Perpetua and Felicity. The boy assented, but warned that the moths were sometimes hard to find, and when found sometimes hard to control. The boy watched over Brother Filippo as he packed the food into the satchels astride the little mule, and Brother Filippo was both angry and grateful for the boy's help in resisting gluttony. The boy ventured they begin by walking down the road to the city, for the moths would not know the construction finished and walls closed, and thusly might walk up the road toward the Priory as so oft they did.

The stars did not mind the boy's attention to the mule or their missed exercising, and were content to their Feast Day rest. The three pilgrims walked halfway to the city when heard they the moths flapping, heading up the road to the Priory just as the boy had guessed. The moths were joyful to reunite with the boy, and even happier to see Brother Filippo had brought them a feast. The boy, too, joyed at the reunion. He was unsurprised to see the eclipse smaller than it was previous, knowing that several of the moths would have been taken by the winter, as they were every year. He remembered the small boy who died under the warm stars.

The pack yelped in protest when Brother Filippo announced that the food and clothing would be distributed only after finished he his sermon on Perpetua and Felicity. The boy worried, but in his presence the wolves bayed. He was not as old as the oldest of them, but now he was stronger than all.

Brother Filippo stood upon a pine stump and preached the story of the African mistress Perpetua and her pregnant slave girl Felicity, the story of two women bound across different stations by their faith, arrested together when they refused to renounce it. Roman law forbad execution of pregnant women, requiring suspension until after birth, yet the Romans did not know Felicity was pregnant. Felicity prayed God delay the birth so that she and her mistress and the unborn child could be martyred together. God granted her prayers, and the three were together devoured by wild animals in the coliseum of Rome.

The story caused the boy think of the stars, of Aquila, of imperfect prayers by men made perfect by God, and of wild and unwild animals. It made the moths think only of devouring Brother Filippo's food, and possibly more.

The sermon complete and the food and clothing equably distributed, Brother Filippo ended the feast announcing the church construction done and the Priory walls closed. The boy saw in the moths' eyes what was always there: the knowledge that pleasure for them only made their suffering worse, that good luck was a sprinkle of dew in rivers of bad, and that life for them would nary change. The boy also saw in the eyes of a few of the larger moths gleams of desire and villainy. *Who knows what delights this fat man hides under his warm brown cowl? The cowl itself would be worth his death. And the meat from that scrawny mule could feed us for weeks.*

The boy retrieved from his rucksack a thick oak rod he found riding the walls with the stars, and a great rusty knife half-sword in dimensions he found in the tower of refuse. He hit the two together innocent, as if he were trying to knock the rust off the knife. He said naught, but saw the greed and villainy drain. After saying farewells, the eclipse flew back down the road and toward the city, and away from their walled-out good fortune.

Life for the boy continued apace. The chapel frescoes sang but did not mystify, the men on the north wall stayed clear and bewildering, the piece of wall stayed mute, and the boy and the stars grieved Aquila. Their grief was tempered for a short while by excitement for the coming Feast of St. Thomas Aquinas.

35

Each year, to celebrate Aquinas, bonfires would bedight the road to the city, and each year the friars would on horseback lead a night parade down to the city and back. The Prior regular borrowed the horses from farmers of the local parish, who were always eager to lend, but this year he had the stars. There were seventeen friars, one was ill, and so they were in need only of five farmers' horses. Each year, the Prior would lead the parade on the largest and whitest steed the farmers could produce, making a fierce competition amongst them. But this year the Prior had the stars.

On the day of the parade, during the Prior's regular visit of inquiry, he made a startling announcement to the boy. He would ride Cassiopeia in the parade. "Yet," the boy said protesting though smiling in wonder, "she is the smallest of the stars, almost just a mule."

"But knows she the secrets of this painting and its silent child, and if we coax her perhaps be she will tell them. And you will join us, riding astride, on the star you pick." The boy chose Canis Minor, for she was the second smallest and would not tower when next to little Cassiopeia.

The boy explained the stars that all of them would be in the parade, and asked them to forgive the Prior for selecting one above all, and to forgive the boy for selecting Canis Minor above the rest, but they sang that their spirits would all at the front of the column be and that all was well. The boy also begged the mule forgiveness for the abandonment by all, but the mule neither objected nor even seemed to notice.

The boy could see the farmers angry when the Prior led the parade on the tiny mare, yet the Prior postured as if he were riding the most important horse in all Christendom. The boy could also see the friars angry that an orphan boy living in the Priory stables should ride in the parade, and at the Prior's side. No outsider had in the friars' memory ever been allowed to ride in the Parade of Aquinas. The friars began whispering what they had long been thinking: this boy is the Prior's bastard son out of one of those mountain slatterns at the convent, perhaps even that harridan Mother Superior herself, who, after all, so recent visited the boy and the Prior.

The parade was glorious, and the stars and the men on the wall all seemed the brighter upon its completion. Perhaps, the boy reckoned, the stars had drawn light from the miles of bonfires, and shared the light with the men on the wall.

The Prior soon became aware of the friars' slanderous stirrings, as good priors become, and he ruminated this latest twist in his political difficulties. He could not allow these rumors spread and infect the fellowship of the Priory. He had seen this agone, and the infection and death were quick as pox. Yet he could not tell the truth of the boy, for that truth would lead to the painting on the wall, and the inundation of the miracle seekers. The Prior prayed God for answer, but it did not come upon the moment of prayer. Yet come it did freely, and without reckonings, when next the Prior and boy spoke and the boy inquired of grief. This, thought the Prior, is the nature of prayer. God always answers, yet in His own time.

After reporting as ever that yea, the painting on the wall is consistent clear, and that nay, the wall on the door has not cleared, and that nay, he would not to move to the Priory, the boy inquired the Prior whether grief was always equal in length to the amount of erstwhile love, and why so he was still grieving Aquila. This was the gate God sent delayed, the opening to quell the friars' defamatory rumbles. The Prior said to the boy, "Well, do still you grieve for your father, dead so long ago?"

"I never knew my father, Prior, so I have never grieved his death only his absent life."

"He was not absent, he was dead."

Then the Prior told the story of the boy's father, not the whole river of story but enough to navigate the shoals of falsehood and pandemonium. He told the boy his father was a wealthy artisan from another city, who met his mother, the daughter of a merchant from the city here, whilst he travelled to work in the cathedral. The two fell quick and hard in love, but the girl's father would nary consent to marriage, for he objected to out-of-towners and also to artisans. The two trothed over the objections, losing the entirety of the girl's dowry. "The man, your father, was killed months ere you were born, in a duel fought over your mother's honor. She died giving life to you. Because your mother's family disinherited her, and because your father's brothers successfully fought his testament and likewise disinherited you, there was none to care for you. Your father's servants brought you here, and I brought you to the convent orphanage."

"Why so have you not told me this previous?" the boy asked.

"There is no substance to tell. Never I knew the names of the two families, and the artisans and merchants buzzing round the cathedral in those times were so great in number it would have been impossible to find them. Moreover, neither family wanted finding, the true measure of orphanage."

The Prior reached out to comfort the boy, placing his arm upon the boy's shoulders. "In fact, let us soon hold a special Mass to honor your nameless mother and father. We will invite the sisters, and perhaps even the Mother Superior would attend." The Prior correctly guessed this would satisfy the boy temporary, and would twinly solve the problem of the rebelling friars.

In three days' time the Mass was held. The Mother Superior attended and even spoke words of comfort to the boy, loud for all to hear. "I knew your father and mother, boy, not by name but by their character, and they were blessed people scythed ere they could enjoy the blessing of their beloved child. I think of them every day, and pray for them and for you. This Mass is far too long in coming," and she fired an accusing glance at the Prior.

These were more words than anyone had ever heard formed by the Mother Superior's lips. Unbeknownst to the hearing, she spoke them under the Prior's hidden pressures, for the Prior knew more secrets of more people than anyone north of the Po. Yet the pressures were not so great to bend the heart of the words false.

The friars were satisfied. God in heaven could not command the Mother Superior speak any falsehood, least one about her own beloved orphanage, and least during the holy Mass. All was well, as long as the secrets of the men on the wall remained sealed.

Chapter 5

The Twelfth Star

The day following this special Mass remembering his unknown parents, the boy managed to steal some time from the selfsame painter in the chapel to whom his earlier intentions were prevented. The boy's intention now was to discover more about his artisan father, but he decided to start crooked by asking the painter of his materials and methods.

The boy learned the painter an apprentice in the very studio of the family of masters whose grandfather produced the fresco of the crucifixion on the south wall of the stables, the boy's poor lonely roommate with whom he never spoke. The apprentice, just a boy himself, was proud to answer questions about his craft. None had ever asked him about his craft, or even named what he did with the appellation of craft, for he was a lowly apprentice, sent to these chapels only to do some small touching up work far below the stations of his masters.

To maintain the deviation, the boy asked the apprentice about the soul of painting, about the difference of surfaces that sang only of beauty and those through whom truth also sang, the queries he had originally planned for the apprentice ere this news of his artisan father. In his excitement of the approaching visage of his dead father, the boy mentioned the painting on the north wall of the stables, that he could see the painting clear though to others it was almost vanished, that he saw edges with no lines and shadowed shapes holding within them both beauty and truth, and that all these visions were best seen in total darkness. His excitement about his approaching father had driven away the Prior's admonitions that the boy was never to speak of the painting nor of his visions.

The apprentice was awestruck, as much by the boy's profound questions as by his claimed visions, certain the two were of one, and the boy some young master disguised by God or Satan for trickery. The apprentice told the boy, truthfully, that he did not know the answers to these questions but that he oft pondered them. By the time the boy got to his questions about the artisans at the city's cathedral, the apprentice was reeling still from the boy's mystery, thinking about what he should tell his masters of it, and brusquely told the boy he knew nay out-of-town artisans or of anyone who did, which was true.

When the boy confessed to the Prior that he had forgotten the admonitions of secrecy, and told the apprentice of the painting and his visions, the Prior grew angry, yet the flash soon cooled to worry. The Prior knew the apprentice was teasing a hole in the web of secrets, that if the miracle seekers came, come they would through this apprentice. The Prior made new plans to weir the flood from Rome, and prayed God none would come from Seville.

The day following, the apprentice, now himself trying to extract information from the boy ere reporting the fantastic tale to his masters, began to teach the boy of painting. The boy, still deceiving for news of his father, feigned interest in the lessons. Yet over time the feigning turned true. Soon the turning became an obsession that even doused the boy's fire to learn of his father.

The apprentice taught the boy to mix pigments with flax to make the paint. Then suggested he lessons in drawing, perspective, and proportion, yet the boy told he knew what he must paint, so the apprentice proceeded with a lesson on the different brushes, how to load the paint upon them, how to mix the paints to produce offspring of a thousand colors. He offered to show the boy how to work the paint into plaster for fresco, yet the boy averred he was interested only in painting upon dry plaster, not painting with wet. The apprentice cautioned that such process would never stand time, yet the boy insisted. When the apprentice explained that it took a lifetime to master the art of painting, the boy thanked him and told that he believed he had learned sufficient. The lessons were done.

As cleaned they the brushes and paint drippings, the apprentice asked the boy describe what he could see of the painting on the north wall of the stables, yet this time the boy remembered the Prior's warning. "Alas," the boy lied, "I was jesting about that painting, only in order to extract your painterly instructions." The apprentice did not believe him, but clapped the boy's ears to feign irritation.

The boy's dreams of painting his visions were blocked by two boulderous truths. He had nay coins for paintly supplies, and his beloved painting upon the north wall still bore the gash of the door. The boy reasoned the Prior might assist with the former, but perceived no solution to the latter. So the boy kept his learnings of pigment and brushes, and his dreams of recreating the painting, as stored seeds, waiting for God's warmth and water.

The boy's daily exercise of the horses warmed the Prior's spirits. Oft he would open the window of the study so to hear the trotting and occasional galloping cross the grounds. One day, contemplating the meaning of the horses and their connection to the paintings on the wall and door, the Prior's mind wandered to the arithmetic of the boy's daily routine.

Scheduling the workouts for eleven horses would be much more difficult than those of twelve, not only because twelve was the number of hours in the light of day but also because no number could divide eleven, whereas many numbers divided twelve. Had there been twelve horses, the boy could spend one third hour exercising each, and be finished in exactly four hours. But how to parcel the time amongst eleven?

These mathematical musings soon exploded into an answer. Twelve was the answer that connected the mystery of the horses with the mystery of the faded painting on the door. Twelve did not explain either mystery, but connected them.

Much as the boy just a few days ere had pounded on the Prior's door to enlighten him, now Prior would enlighten boy. He instructed the befuddled Brother Bartolomeo to ride the fastest star to the city and acquire a new horse, without saddle, and lead the new horse to the stables. The new horse was to be a large roan gelding, matching as possible the visage of Aquila, yet Bartolomeo was to spend no more than three reals. The old servant grumbled but complied.

When returned Brother Bartolomeo with a fine horse in tow, though grey not roan, the Prior applauded the old servant's work then alighted himself upon Cassiopeia, taking the new grey horse in tow. The Prior galloped the two horses along the wall in search of the boy. He found him far at the west wall rubbing down one of the stars, whose name the Prior did not know, for he recognized only Cassiopeia and Ursa Major. He told the boy of his discovery, introduced the boy to his newest star, and boy and man upon two horses, the other being Canis Minor, led the new third and galloped to the stables.

The boy returned Canis Minor to his place amongst the stars, but instead of putting the leads now on Pisces, as was the boy's unalterable custom, he introduced the twelfth horse. The others startled first at the changed pattern then at the new horse, but soon established. Ere the boy continued with the exercises, the Prior explained this horse had been named Trident, but that the boy could name it as he pleased. The boy had already decided on a name on the ride back to the stables. His name would be Moon, for the light that shone only sometimes, the light that illuminated but did not blind.

And illuminate it did. Prior and boy knew it would not happen that night. But the morning following the next, still in Matins, for the Prior's patience could not wait even until Lauds, sat the Prior in the stables on a bale of hay as the boy described the clarifying shapes on the door wall. These were indeed the tall man's feet, crossed under the table, a ribbon of red tunic showing from under the blue cape. This segment also revealed two more slats in the floor, two more sets of table legs, and some small bits of other men's feet. The boy wept at the reunion, and the Prior wept at the boy's description of the reunion. As with the mother, the new child grew clearer and clearer each night. Indeed, once Moon joined the stars, the two grew together even brighter and clearer.

When the tears dried, the boy told the Prior his plan. He would find another large piece of discarded plaster, and he would paint upon it the images he saw on the door. If this achieved well, he would recreate the entire painting on another wall of the stables— the west wall would have to do since the doors of the east wall would intrude. The Prior wept at this grand idea, wept at the prospect that the whole painting might one day be revealed to him.

It was also a clever idea. The painting hidden in the stables could be hidden without hiding, just as its predecessor. Even if someone happened into the stables, the stars would be gathered at the west wall and none would gaze that direction but to ready a horse, and then not upward looking to the heights of the new painting.

The Prior and the boy gave short discussings to the boy using the south wall, to have him cover the painting of the crucifixion, but both concluded this would displease God, for surely it was a sin for one painter to destroy the work of another. And of course neither would have proposed covering the mysterious original with the boy's copy. For the same reason, the boy must recreate the test painting from the door, not just paint over it.

Yet the Prior remained worried of this plan. Word of the recreated masterpiece and of this new master would certain bring the locusts of miracle. But he so longed to see what the boy saw that he relented against these wise fears. He gave the boy money to purchase pigments and other supplyings, and sent him to the city with Brother Filippo to accomplish the transactions, to begin the first step of the great miracle.

43

Brother Filippo rode Ursa Major, the only star strong enough to carry the mountain such distance. The boy rode his new Moon. Brother Filippo told to the pigment merchant that the Prior of the little church and priory to the west had commissioned a new painting, that this boy was the painter's servant, and that the boy knew what pigments were needed. The merchant asked the name of his master, yet the boy said he was sworn to secrecy, and that all he could say was that he was a famous out-of-town painter. After the boy selected the pigments, brushes, and flax, the merchant offered him plaster, but the boy explained that this would be nay fresco, that his master would paint upon wood. The merchant offered special treatments for wood painting, yet the boy declined, for of course he knew yet could not say he would be painting upon plaster.

At their return, the boy took Moon and scoured the grounds for another large piece of wall. Now that construction was complete, the boy worried that all of the large pieces would have been long broken or burnt. He searched first near the peat mounds, now in late winter all but gone, and then in a moment of inspiration took Moon to the junction of the walls where Cassiopeia first found the piece of wall. Still they found naught.

In a second inspiration, the boy returned to the stables, blanketed Cassiopeia, and put a pack saddle on the mule. Just as the boy hoped, and just as the little girl had done afore, Cassiopeia walked straight to her destination, this time north and west, to the pines across the short exposure of mountain stream that disappeared to feed the well. She stopped at a large pine, against which sat a felled relative.

The boy looked round for plaster, yet saw none. He scolded Cassiopeia for her mistake and tried to lead her away, but she would not move. The boy dismounted and looked at the trees with increased care. The felled tree had split, and down under half of her, nestled against the standing pine, was a giant but thin slab of pine, one side so smooth it looked as if it had been hewn. Two of its corners were even slight rounded, mimicking the kitchen door. The boy had planned to paint on plaster as the master of the north wall had done, but Cassiopeia and God had other ideas. The boy hoisted the pine slab onto the mule's pack saddle, securing it with ropes, and the expedition returned to the stables.

Now that the work was to be on pine not plaster, the boy begged Brother Filippo return to the city pigment merchant and acquire the special wood treatments earlier offered, and Brother Filippo joyfully agreed. He loved riding Ursa Major, loved riding any horse, as all blacksmiths secretly do. The merchant suspicioned how the apprentice to such famous artist would decline the special wood tincture one day only to request it the next, and so inquired. Brother Filippo, as the Prior instructed in anticipation, explained that the boy errantly believed his master had sufficient tincture yet discovered this morn it all but gone. The merchant accepted, inquired of the size of the painting to assess the needed quantity of tincture, and sold four large vials.

As the false apprentice never permitted the true to teach the manner of application of these special treatments, the Prior devised Brother Filippo extract the information from the merchant by innocent conversation. Indeed, this is why so the boy did not join in this second trip. As instructed, by way of feigned complaining about travel to the city a second time, Brother Filippo made talk to the merchant about the need for such treatment, what a painting upon wood would endure without it, and how exact to apply it. As instructed, Brother Filippo careful memorized the application lessons, and told them to the boy upon his return.

The boy began the painting on the Feast of the Annunciation, and worked through the night. He propped the wooden slab immediately astride the kitchen door mounted with the visions of the feet. He treated the wood with the tincture in the manner related him by Brother Filippo, then, with the treatment dry and sanded, traced the images with a small brush loaded with faint yellow almost invisible against the pine. He painted in total darkness, for total darkness made the visions clearest.

The darkness prevented him from seeing his brush at the moment he was applying the paint, but the instant paint was upon the wood it revealed itself as his visions had revealed. Likewise, the darkness required the boy mix the colors on the painting itself, rather than on a palette separate. He arranged the small pots of paint in a strict order committed to his memory, for the darkness also blinded him to their color. In the beginning, ere his memory of the paints was firm, he laughed aloud as he looked up and saw the tall man had a blueish rightmost foot, the boy having mistaken the pots of blue and brown.

The Prior ordered the boy not disturbed, and Brother Bartolomeo placed his meals at the stable doors, yet the meals went uneaten. The stars, who were patterned to their daily exercise, skittished at first at their inactivity, yet over time they too settled to the task of miracle. Even when the painting had long been finished, for it took him only that single night, the boy spent hours staring at it and measuring it to what he saw on the door. He changed nary a nit, but it took him two days to content with what he had not changed. He ate during these long days of staring, and the Prior was pleased at Brother Bartolomeo's report that the meals were now being consumed.

Shortly before Prime on the third day, the boy pounded on the Prior's study door. When Brother Bartolomeo opened the door and gained him entrance, neither the Prior nor boy spoke. The Prior looked at the boy in reverence and the boy nodded reverently. The two walked silent to the stables, and an uninvited Brother Bartolomeo trailed behind.

The boy himself had of course already been seized by the painting, yet to see others seized was even more beautiful. And to have others seized merely by this tiny part, a part that contained none of the agonized faces the boy saw, was more beautiful still. The boy was also prideful that he was capable of such work, albeit also confused at the source of his capacities. The Prior, though looking only at some legless crossed feet draped in blue over a band of red, a few slats and table legs, and two disembodied feet, collapsed in veneration. Brother Bartolomeo, too, was moved, yet less palpably.

The boy invited the Prior remove the painting to his office, for the boy was in no need of two. With Moon now joined to the stars, the boy could gaze at the crossed feet freely all nights. The Prior agreed, and though the boy could have carried the painting himself, for pine wood is considerable lighter than plaster, the Prior instructed Brother Bartolomeo to assist the boy, and into the Prior's study the two brought the painting, covered with the boy's beetle holey blankets.

The Prior directed them hang the painting on the wall opposite the study window. Brother Bartolomeo recruited Brother Filippo to assist. Brother Filippo stared at the Christ's legs but did not weep, looking back and forth tween them and the boy. The Prior directed them move the large tapestry that covered the north wall, depicting the resurrection, to cover the painting, but to fix the tapestry only at its topmost edge, and fashion it with a rope so that it could be raised to reveal the painting and lowered to conceal it. When the work was done, the Prior raised the tapestry and the three men and boy stood and gazed at the painting until the bells for Prime brought them back. Now Brother Filippo was weeping, his hand upon the boy's head.

At that moment of the bells, the Prior remembered that the boy could see the whole of the painting, and yearned to see it with him. He undertook commission of the boy to repaint what he saw, on whatever material and at whatever location the boy saw fit, no matter the cost. The Prior now could see the boy's destiny approaching his own, and gave thanks to God. But the Prior was also of the world, and fretted of the secrets and of a newly copied painting revealing them. Yet he must see it. He prayed God again to keep the secrets.

Chapter 6

The Masters and Signorie

Two days hence, a caravan of three old men and one young reached the Priory gate. They had not sent forward a message, for they knew their reputations would gain them entrance. They were the master painters of the city, brothers, accompanied by their apprentice, the selfsame apprentice who schooled the boy of painting. The masters' great-grandfather and great-uncles had painted murals and frescos in the cathedral, and their grandfather had painted the fresco of the crucifixion in the forgotten refectory of this forgotten little priory.

Their grandfather would have visited regularly, and bathed this little place in his great fame, had the feckless friars not converted the refectory into stables, thusly consigning the timeless work to be adored only by horses and their stink. The great painter conveyed his distain to his children, and they to theirs, and thusly did the grandchildren masters have no reason to visit this remote dung hole, and never did so former. Indeed, when the Prior of this place recent inquired to commission work from them on the chapels, they said they were too busy but could send their apprentice yet for the same master price, and the gullible cleric agreed. But now, the wild claims of their apprentice, and history's undeserved judgment of the Florentine cretin who painted the ruined fresco opposite, piqued them curious.

Alas, their reputation was not great enough to entreat the brothers at the gate to allow them entrance, so one of the gate brothers left to inquire of the Prior. When finally to the Prior's study the artly men were admitted, they spied a space filled with third-class paintings and second-class furnishings, though their apprentice was more charitable in his silent judgment of the paintings. The masters minced nay words. "A boy works here who claims visions of the dissolved fresco opposite our grandfather's. Is he mad or a witch? We demand his presence for inquiry."

The Prior had prayed against this news, but twinly planned for it. "The poor boy, starved, has gone mad. We have sent him and his suffering soul to a churchly house for mental feebles in Lyon." The masters nodded and whispered.

"We will see our grandfather's fresco now, to assure its maintenance." The Prior predicted this request, and wisely sent Brother Bartolomeo to the stables to hide evidence of the boy's tenancy and retire the boy to the root cellar. The Prior led the masters and their apprentice to the stables, all the time the masters shaking their heads that their grandfather's masterpiece should be so rurally enshrined. They looked at the fresco in awe, then upon close inspections with candled light, though it was day and the stables moderate bright from the opened doors and the light leaking betwixt rafters and walls.

The masters discussed with one another in close detail divers technical aspects of the fresco, and seemed general satisfied at its condition, though they did demand more regular and careful cleaning. Instructed they the Prior on the details of such cleaning, its materials and methods and frequency. The Prior smiled and nodded as if to undertake these directions, yet spoke not for would he not to commit the sin of falsehood.

"And here," the Prior volunteered, pointing to the wall behind, "you can see that this wall has been flaked almost clean.

This is the wall upon which the poor mad boy imagined, in his ravings, a complete and colorful painting." The masters turn round, clucked, and shook their heads.

"But I taught him to paint," said the apprentice at first shyly, "and said he that he would to paint on dry plaster, just as Leonardo did here." The masters glared at this naming of the undeserved Florentine who was never to be named. "What has the boy painted?" asked the apprentice of the Prior, now more boldly.

"Naught. The poor boy's desire to paint and his claimed visions of this dissolved painting each sprang as twins from his madness," explained the Prior. The masters, yet not the apprentice, seemed satisfied.

The threads of secret were unravelling, the Prior reckoned, as he bid away the fulsome men and their troubling apprentice. He would pray St. Nonnatus that the boy's secrets remain sealed. Aye, though Nonnatus, the never-born, was but canonized less three score years ago, the Prior reasoned the selfsame newness would leave the pup saint energized to solve the gnarl. And what better saint to protect the never born boy than a saint never born, each cut from their mothers? Perhaps he would celebrate Nonnatus with a feast. He consulted his filled Book of Days, marveling at its fullness.

The Prior garish celebrated more feast days in this little outpost than the Pope himself. His first feastly order, yet one month from his posting, was to St. Brendan, protector of sailors, for the Prior was a sailing man ere God's winds found him. He consulted the texts for guidance, found none, and thusly scripted the feast himself, naming it "The Feast of St. Brendan's Waterly Protection." He bid the brothers drape the outer walls in blue tapestries, being the seas, and the campanile in white ones, being the sails of a ship, showing to all townspeople and near farmers that St. Brendan would carry the ships of God's creatures safely. He directed a parade of brothers and friars round the outside of the walls, the friars holding long spikes of pine, being oars, and the brothers rolling casks showing of rum, but being of the Priory's wine, which was then drunk by all in celebration.

Here, more than a century of miles from any sea, the towns-people and farmers yet loved the parade, and cast it as protection against the floods of the Seveso and Lambro. The brothers alike loved the fete and especially the rivers of charity wine. The friars grumbled about their new master, the seriousness of his soul and the heaviness of his purse.

Their grumbles were rewarded with a storm of feasts never celebrated to any resident's memory. There was the Feast of St. Adrian, for the Prior to invoke protections for soldiers, yet which he turned as a shield against pox and plague. He marched with every shepherd and their flocks in his Feast of St. Drago, four hours up to the convent and orphanage and four back, leaving several lambs for the sisters. During his Feast of St. Timothy, the Prior distributed throughout the town vialed tinctures he learned in his navying days to invoke against bad achings of the stomach. And for his Feast of St. Catherine of Bologna, his brothers carried his paintings from the Priory through the town, that the people could know the mystery and glory of God's artly renderings. Sundry more fetes did he script.

There were so many newly feasts that the friars accelerated their whisperings of the Prior's fortune and the means by which he had gained it. The Prior, learning of these rumblings, parried by scribing a short text, bound with leatherings, that told true the erstwhile story of his birthing and rearing in Genoa, of his wealthy merchant father, of the drowning of all but he as the family sailed to Barcelona, of his inheritance of the family's treasure, and of his callings to the sea and to God. He ended the scripting with praise of the vow of poverty, undertaking formally to use his monies for good churchly works. He did not command the friars read it, nay, he knew that by not so commanding all of them would read, and too would find it true. And they did read and so find, and the rumblings of ill-gotten gains ceased.

Yet the Prior had commissioned so many newly feasts that now he troubled placing St. Nonnatus into the listings. Yea, the Church's Proper of Saints was permanent full, oft three or four saints each day. Yet the Prior's fancy showings required many days of costly preparation, and thusly could not land close. The texts reported Nonnatus's day the last of August, yet the Prior had just commissioned the 24th of that selfsame month for the Feast of Saint Bartholomew, patron of plasterers. Still, the Prior persisted. Two feasts with only one week betwixt were extreme, yet the extremity could be salved by making them both reverent and understated.

His newest creation, for the protector of plasterers, would not even include a marching out of the walls. The Prior would commission Brother Filippo make a large mixture of plaster, and all the friars would circumvallate the interior of the walls in repairs, praying continuously for the miracle of plaster. The Prior smiled. The friars would not appreciate this quiet and laboring internal Feast, which might all the more increase the others in their view.

His plasterly designs for the Feast of St. Bartholomew caused the Prior also to revise the script of the traditional Feast of St. Luke, past celebrated each October 25 only with a special mass. This year, the Prior would again direct Brother Filippo make plaster, two large mixtures, one divided into seven pots and one remained whole. The Prior would commission the boy and his horses Cassiopeia and Moon hunt the Priory grounds, and even afar if need be, for large slabs of pine akin the one behind the tapestry holding the Christ's feet. He would commission the boy lath the pine with the plain plaster and pigment the small pots each with a different color. Then he would direct all the friars to the brushes and fresco knives and order them to fresco. And thusly the first revised Feast of St. Luke would celebrate with the friars making their own artly creations upon God's creation of wood and plaster.

The Prior mused both at the imagined creating and at the imagined creations. He knew many friars would be troubled by the expectations, for they had never to any surface put any markings save to copy texts with ink upon parchment. As sailors never in water, the Prior thought, but the wetness will make good of them. And reveling in God's gift of art was true and good, aye, even the artless might revel most. Some would remain fretted, and complain at the madness of their spendthrift Prior possessed by artly creation, but in the whole the company would uplift.

The Prior arrested these musings, for much more pressing was the scripting of St. Nonnatus. His day was seven days ere the day of St. Bartholomew and months ere the day of St. Luke, yet Nonnatus was not scripted. Returning to the texts, the Prior was unsurprised of no guidance for one so new as St. Never Born. Glad of heart, began he to write for this new August feast, warmed by thoughts of an end to the never-ending cold.

Even as he was scratching preparations for the summer celebration, a messenger from the city brought a cold demand. The city's signorie were requesting for an audience to discuss rumors of the stable boy who could give vision to the Florentine's masterpiece. These days, the signorie's requests were more akin commands, propped by distant but ever-present Spanish power.

They arrived the day following the request, ere the Prior's response. The brothers at the gate recognized their red silks and jangling silver and admitted them without word. Five of them there were, each portly and bejeweled and of serious countenance. The boy spied them as he returned Centaurus from exercise. He watched as they dismounted their exhausted horses and made their way to the Priory, entering after knocking but ere granted Brother Bartolomeo's permission.

The fat men huddled round the wide hearth rubbing their hands and feet warm, dropping mud on the fine rug the Prior bought in Cairo in his sailing years. Even as the rubbings and droppings continued, the signorie began their inquiries.

They reported they learned of this magic from an apprentice of their city's master painters, and, as they knew the masters themselves had done, they demanded both explanation of the boy and visitation of the painting. Again, Brother Bartolomeo retired to secret the boy in the root cellar, and again the Prior explained the boy was mad and in a house of lunatics in Lyon. Again, the Prior led the men to the stables, where they shook their heads in disappointment, gazing on the ruined masterpiece.

"Our dear Duke, rest his soul, promised this charlatan a fortune, and the mountebank's labors lasted longer than his product," one of the signorie said, starting but resisting a sweep of his hand to flake off more plaster.

One of the signorie had brought a poor copy of the painting, which he used to map the flakings on the original. So famous was this dissolved masterpiece that poorly copied offspring abounded in the city and across the land, yet their poorness was not imagined for none living had ever see the mother. Yet having gazed only upon Christ's feet, through the exactness of the boy's copy, the Prior near collapsed in renewed awe of the imagined original. The signorie did not notice.

"If only the boy truly saw, and could tell the masters what he saw, and they repaint this, think of the renewed trade to the city!"

"Even if he did not truly see, perhaps his imaginings could attend the masters to repaint this masterpiece on the walls of the commune, for all to travel to see," said another.

"Nay," said their leader, "the boy was mad, his imaginings mad, and thusly his attending to the masters would be mad and their rendering a madly abomination. Moreover, our city masters are not as masterful as they boast, for their family's genius has withered considerable across the generations. But these talks have me to think might we raise a new tax to inspire some Florentine, or in best dreaming even a Venetian, to make the finest rendering of this great masterpiece, placed in the commune, and thereby increase the prominence of our fine city. After all, copies abound, thus it is not the case that what was here is unknown though the place itself has become unknown."

The signorie contented themselves with these commercial discussions and repaired from the Priory without even glancing upon the crucifixion on the south wall, still conversing on their topic, saying naught to the Prior, who returned to his summer plannings and to St. Never Born.

Chapter 7

The Bishops and Archbishop

Whilst churches across the land readied their observances of Ash Wednesday, the Prior held his Feast of John of God, he canonized mere decades hence and great beloved by the Prior for his soldering life and bookselling patronage. Townspeople and farmers all were fed on this day to a meal in the cloister, weather gracing, else in the cleared stables, which, after all, had erstwhile been the refectory. Each year, this generous and gay meal followed with a tour of the Prior's private library, each visitor entreated to borrow one of the books for a season, though this offer was seldom accepted for few could read.

This day the weather was fine yet cool, and the pre-Lenten meal enjoyed in the open air. A farmer's boy even requested a book, yet his father clapped him about the ears for the request. The Prior insisted the boy take the book. It was a book of Copernicus, festooned with intriguing drawings of loops and swirls. The boy cautiously placed his name, of which he knowledged to write, also a rarity, in the tabulations prepared by Brother

Bartolomeo to record the intermittent lendings, casting wary looks first to father then to Prior.

The Prior repeated his permission yet informed the boy with stern brow that the book must be returned by the Feast of St. Boniface. None knew when these peculiar feasts celebrated, and this ignorance was plain on the boy's face. The Prior smiled away from his sternness, and told that St. Boniface would be celebrated June 5. The Prior even wrote this date of return upon a scrap of parchment and placed it into the book, hopeful the scrap would speak to the boy if his memory of the obligation failed.

On Shrove, the Prior directed the brothers gather from the construction piles such plaster dust as they could find and place the dust in sacks, directions unbeknownst to the friars and a mystery of execution to the brothers. Soon, the brothers worked that if they shook a collection of lathed plasters whilst it remained inside a bag, they could afterwords remove the solid parts and be left mostly with the pulver.

Though the Prior clear directed the mission to be secreted from the friars, yet one of the brothers, Brother Vincenzo, he of the love of the grape, squeaked the news to one of the friars, who spread it to all. They were thusly unsurprised when during the communion the Prior sprinkled their heads with white plaster dust in the stead of grey ashes of burnt palms. Unsurprised were all yet angry some at this departure from canon, and the angriest posted to the Archbishop a letter detailing this and other claimed heresies in the Prior's term.

The poster was Friar Ignatius, a dour young man from Granada who arrived at the Priory yet two months ere the Prior himself arrived. Despight the twinness of the languages, Friar Ignatius never mastered Italian, and the few words he could speak were laden heavy with accent. Perhaps this contributed to his outcastedness, which he wore fierce and relentless. Perhaps the arrival of a new superior ignited these smolderings of not belonging. Perhaps his training in Spain, in the womb of St. Dominic and in the shadow of the lunatics in Seville, prepared him ill for the kindness of Italian Dominicans, especially the Prior's feast- and wealth-laden version. Perhaps the young man saw the churchly life as a punishment, as so many unaccepting priests did, and, as punishment begats punishment, lashed out at all for his misfortune. This was the Prior's explanation, for he had oft seen such resentment, especially in the young.

It was yet a month past the Prior's arrival that Friar Ignatius began his complainings, of the Prior's wealth, of his infidelity to the doctrines of the order, of his naming mere servants as Brothers, and especially of his ridiculous theatrical feastings. The Prior had just announced the Feast of St. Brendan, which Friar Ignatius did not sanction and which he told to the other friars was a "pagan celebration of a Viking jacktrap," yet all knew the Spaniard, unschooled in Italian, meant "jacktar."

These complaints, made only to his brethren, yet soon found their way to the Prior, who summoned Friar Ignatius to inquire of his unhappiness. The two first danced civil, yet the Prior broke the ballet by commanding Friar Ignatius explain his words of St. Brendan: "So, a young man raw from seminary knows more truly than our beloved Pope who beatified this 'Viking jacktar'? How do you defend such heresy, boy?" The Prior's saying of the word "heresy" struck the Spaniard cold, but it served only to freshen his hate, which he took care from that day onward to hide in pleasantry. Even his brethren believed the Prior's words had changed the young man, yet they had only drove his unhappiness deep and invisible.

Mere three days past Friar Ignatius's messaging, a churchly column from the city made its way to the Priory. Six priests there were, headed by three bishops astride, themselves headed by the Archbishop himself at point. No Archbishop had ever visited the Priory, and even a mere bishop's visit was rare, least three. The priests wore black and the bishops purple, and thusly the column appeared as a black-bodied and purple-headed white-horned caterpillar, the bishops' white mitres leading and exaggerating the undulations of the advancing creature. The bishops' horns were plain white, bearing red crosses front and back. The Archbishop's horn gleamed with gold, adorned and jeweled so highly that none of the adornments or jewels sang solo yet rather made a chorus. Through the chorus could be heard the double-lined red crosses, front and back.

The poor young brothers at the gate had never previous seen a bishop least an archbishop, and opened they the gate ere the column lay 100 yards from entrance. They kneeled then genuflected then saluted then bowed then pointed to the Priory, unschooled in the procedures for such lofty visitations.

The bishops and Archbishop dismounted, but the priests remained upon their horses, taking the leads of the riderless mounts. The colorful caterpillar thusly turned headless black, and the flowing purple silks entered the Priory without knocking upon its door. The boy saw none of this, as he was in one of the chapels sweeping the final leavings from the constructions. He wondered, as he completed his labors, what next his commission would be, for exercising the stars consumed yet one-half day.

Friar Ignatius saw the entering procession, both surprised and satisfied his missive was so quickly responded. Perhaps, he thought to himself as he took the barrow to the fields to gather peat, the prior next will be of holier more orthodox dedication, perhaps even a Spaniard. Friar Ignatius could not see, and would never have imagined, the transpirings inside the Prior's study.

The Prior knelt and kissed the Archbishop's ring. After formal pleasantries, the Archbishop announced he was appearing not for the Spaniard's complainings, which letter he read aloud to the smiling Prior, but because of claims by a local painter's apprentice of a miracle boy who had visions of the Christ. To this inquiry the Prior laid the same fictions he had lain to the masters and signorie. The boy was stricken with lunacy and had been removed to a madhouse in Lyon. After some private discussings with his bishops, the Archbishop announced he would render this explanation to his texts and close the matter. Then he bid the bishops take meal with the friars whilst he discussed private Church matters with the Prior.

The moment the bishops retired, the Archbishop removed his mitre and the two men embraced, laughing heartily. They were old friends, having sailed both the waters of the Mediterranean and the waters of Church politics for more twenty years. The Archbishop knew from the Prior the truth of the boy's provenance and selection, faithed the truth of his Christ vision, and had travelled to see the boy's rendering of the feet. The Prior pulled up the tapestry and the Archbishop wept. The Prior had gazed upon the feet daily, and thusly the tears emptied dry over time from his awe, yet when he saw the tearful awe in his old friend his own tears returned. This was one of the many wonders of this creation, its power to ignite people in community. The Prior had seen this wonder in other artly works, but nary so blistering as in this.

Once composed, the Archbishop told to the Prior he would himself commission the boy repaint the entirety of the masterpiece, and would pay the materials himself despight the Prior's wealth, for this was a miracle worthy of Archdiocese funding, nay even Papal funding. At mention of the latter the Prior frowned hard, then the Archbishop laughed loud and clapped his friend upon the shoulders. Then undertook he in solemn voice never to speak of the matter to any Roman ears, "even to my brother now serving in Rome," and even though the Archbishop himself was rumored soon for the red cap. He was awealth in power as the Prior was awealth in gold, and the two joked oft about their different and imperfectly congruent treasures.

The Archbishop inquired what he might do for the boy, and the Prior responded the boy was content with his stars, drawing a quizzing from the Archbishop to which the Prior explained the appellation meant the stable workhorses, beloved by the boy. The Prior then told of the connection tween the stars and the painting, the tale never earlier told the Archbishop. The Archbishop shook his head in wonder and genuflected, again gazing at the feet.

The Archbishop told to the Prior that he would officially approve that the repainting be upon the old painting itself. The Prior frowned and told of the technical difficulties, and summoned the boy explain.

The boy had never met a bishop, arch or not. Taken aback by the height of the man augmented by mitre, which the Archbishop had replaced, the boy genuflected and kneeled. The Prior took his arm and raised him, explaining the Archbishop was an old friend to whom the Prior had vouchsafed all the secrets of the boy and stars and vision. The Archbishop removed the bejeweled miter, yet still loomed several hands above the Prior, and embraced the boy warmly.

Then explained the Prior the Archbishop's plans for the re-painting, yet the boy frowned, and said he could not repaint over the masterpiece. The boy told of the flaking plaster, of his miracle skill only in paint and not fresco, and mostly of his belief that to cover the original would be a sin. The Archbishop frowned at the technical explainings yet smiled when the boy explained of the sin.

"Very well, young man, you shall paint the entirety of the masterpiece on large segments of canvas, which I shall procure."

"Your majesty," said the boy, "might I paint upon wood, on pine as I have painted the feet?"

The Archbishop was awed that the feet were upon pine, which he had not former known. He looked again at the feet, genuflected, shook his head, and assented to the boy's request. The three agreed the finished panels should transport to the city, and be watched over there by the Archbishop in a secreted lair in his rectory. The three agreed the panels should be hinged together, so that they might easily be folded for transport and for disguise yet not be lost of another. After excusing the boy, the Prior and Archbishop embraced in farewell, after which the Archbishop spoke that his record would be the end of the matter for Rome, yet cautioned of Seville.

The Prior and the boy laid their plans. The Prior directed that as the boy and Brother Filippo again ride to the city for pigments, concurrent he would commission the carpentering brothers to fashion the five wooden panels. They would be larger than the panel of the feet, for they would run full height, whilst the kitchen door interrupted only half the full height. And they were all to be of full height, for the Archbishop had generously assented that the Prior keep the half-panel of feet for his own, and that the boy re-paint them on the full panels. This pleased the boy, for he worried of knitting the painted feet into the new depiction. It also greatly pleased the Prior, who had fretted at the loss of the beloved feet then prayed forgiveness for his greed. Still, even with the feet in his study, the Prior knew that many a trip to the city he would to take visiting the full painting. Perhaps the number of feast days might reduce to accommodate his new travellings.

The boy reminded the Prior that Cassiopeia could herself discover five apt panels, and there would be no need of carpentry. The Prior, the worldly sailor he, doubted this miracle of the horse and wood could be repeated fives, least with panels of doubled height, yet relented, content that if the horsely quest failed he could commission a craftsmanly one. So Brother Bartolomeo upon Cassiopeia generaled the wooden expedition, whilst Brother Filippo riding Ursa Major and the boy upon Moon set out to the city for the pigments.

The hunt for wood was of considerable less consequence of the two. Brother Bartolomeo genuflected five times at the miracle of the mule-sized horse finding wide and double tall pine panels where never bygone had they been seen. Doubting, like the Prior, that these hunts would find prey, Brother Bartolomeo commissioned only Cassiopeia and not another horse or the mule for pack. Yet wise enough he was, faithful enough, to place a pack saddle upon Cassiopeia in the event the miracle repeated, which was a profound showing of faith as it meant the old bent brother must walk.

When Cassiopeia led to the first panel yet half-an-hour out— thin and perfect as the one for the feet yet twice tall—Brother Bartolomeo wisely returned without the prey, and commissioned the mule for pack, knowing his bent walking would delay both further exploration and delivery. Once Brother Bartolomeo returned upon Cassiopeia with the mule trailing, four more panels Cassiopeia found chock a block, and the strong mule packed all five home.

Yet the hunt for pigment went twisterly. First, Brother Filippo and the boy were confronted by wild dogs less one mile from the Priory walls, though man and boy repelled the pack with loud words and thrown stones. Nextly, the wild dogs of the moths descended upon the two, first with cries of fury until they recognized the boy, then with the hidden fury of hunger when saw they again the fat brother. After pleasantries with the boy, and news of the death of the two eldest boys—hanged for thieving horses in the city—the moth pack receded with reluctance, this time without the need for the boy to show his weapons. The culling of the eldest moths had tamed the swarm.

In the city, the boy again fictioned as the undisclosed master painter's apprentice, and at the selfsame shop before the selfsame merchant they turned the Archbishop's gold into a rainbow of colored packets of pigment, these ten-fold larger than those for the feet. Yet as they bartered with the shop's keeper, the masters' true apprentice spied them, though they not he.

The true apprentice cast his eyes upon the false, the self-same boy the Prior averred to his masters and to the signorie was insane and in Lyon. The selfsame boy who claimed he visioned the disappeared Leonardo. The selfsame boy who was now buying large quantities of pigment. Dismissed bygone by the masters and signorie, the apprentice thought first to lodge his newly evidenced claims with the Church, unawares his masters had taken the case to the Archbishop. Nay, the apprentice corrected his thinking, the Prior had conspired with the boy, and the Prior was church powerful and rich. Nay, the apprentice would lodge his claims with those mastered in the craft of miracles and heresy. He would travel to Seville.

Yet the apprentice had no money. He again entreated his masters to believe him, and his report of the reappeared boy and further pigments turned their minds. How dare this backwater priest lie to them? They commissioned the apprentice travel to Seville, to lodge his tales with the official inquirers of such things. The fires of the Inquisition had dimmed to embers in these years, yet as with some determined fires these flared with surprising heat ere they went full cold.

Chapter 8

Soldiers of the Black Fire

The boy painted the great miracle in the stables as he had painted the smaller, alone but for the stars, who seemed special contented at the project, and the mule, who ignored everything. This was in accordance with the Prior's notion that the best manner of hiding the activity was to hide it where no others went.

The painting proceeded as had the missing feet, the boy painting at night in total darkness when the vision was clearest, seeing the new paint only as it was applied, and memorizing the colors in the invisible pots. The boy began on the leftmost panel, and proceeded by leaning the empty panel against the north wall immediately below its full vision. The boy realized soon he could not transition from one panel to next without the next, the painting being of one whole and not five parts. Thusly the boy requested the Prior bring him the second panel as well, and was able thereby to paint the vision that straddled the two. Likewise the boy painted the remaining, two panels at a time, one half-completed and joined with a blank, each propped up against the north wall below its corresponding vision.

When asked the Prior when he would sleep, the boy told the miracle of the painting required nay sleep, and that in all events he needed keep exercising the stars in a show of routine, so to keep his painting actions secret. The Prior assented.

Discussed they whether the Prior would absent himself as he had done with the feet, but the Prior resisted this tradition, so consumed he was to witness the miracle unfold. Yet the Prior only gentle pushed, and the boy admitted as the Prior's presence might interfere with the paintly application. Besides, the boy reminded, he painted in utter darkness, and the Prior would see naught without candling, and the light from the candle would diminish the boy's visions.

So the two alloyed a compromise: each day shortly ere the bells of Prime, the Prior would visit the boy's progress donned in a brother's robes for disguise. They also agreed that after the inspection and ere the boy exercised the stars, the two would lean the panels severe upright against the wall, painted surfaces facing wall, so that the last painted could freely dry and also so that should any wander into the stables they would not discover. Indeed, the unhewn backs of the panels disappeared into the other rough lumbers in the stables, and even those knowing to look would not see.

The Prior fathomed slivers of progress on his first morning visitation, calculated on the days the boy spent on the feet, unknowing that all save one of those days the boy spent gazing at the done feet. The Prior wept at the sight of the completed left panel and some beginnings on the next, after just one night's work. This was yet more wonder. Wonder upon wonder. Not satisfied with the miracle of creation, God had added the miracle of speed. At the present rate the entire painting would be finished by Holy Monday.

Yet the wonder of speed paled to the wonder of substance. The Prior awed at the gentle shadows that defined the men's tortured and unbelieving faces. Unlike the boy, he knew what agonizing news had been at that moment laid upon them. The miracle deepened to oceans each time the Prior gazed upon a new panel. How so had the master captured those interiors, and how so had the boy recaptured them? The Prior's tears were caught by the up-turns of his faithful and knowing smile.

His ecstasies so great, he was bursted with desire to share the paintings with his beloved Bartolomeo and perhaps even with the lug Filippo, rewards for their assistance. He counseled of the boy on these matters, and the boy was joyed at the proposed sharing, and said of no concerns either brother would vouchsafe the secret.

At this time, the painting was full three panels ending in the previous seen feet now crowned anew with the Christ's body and head, coupled to the beginning scratchings on a fourth. The Prior, disguised as usual in brothers' robes, himself brought Bartolomeo and Filippo to the stables ere Prime, to cast their eyes upon the broadened miracle. Brother Bartolomeo wept as he had wept at the feet, but Brother Filippo froze silent at the face of the Christ. The Prior grew concerned at his unmoving state, and yet more concerned when the mountain collapsed to the straw on the stable floor. Brother Filippo revived, yet could not from the Christ's eyes avert his. The Prior and Brother Bartolomeo assisted him from the stables, all six eyes lingering.

When the miracle was complete, the Prior sent Bartolomeo, on fast Cassiopeia, to the city to message the Archbishop. The message contained but one word: Finished. The Archbishop and one priest whom he trusted arrived the day next disguised as travelling monks. One of the gate brothers inquired of the Prior ere bidding the two in, for these days many highwaymen disguised as hooded monks. Upon the Prior's assent, the monks entered and dismounted, one of the gate brothers leading their horses to paddock, and approached the Priory. The shorter monk remained outside as Bartolomeo escorted the larger inside. Once within the study, the Archbishop re-robed as a Brother of the Priory and the Prior joined the misleading wardrobe, and both walked unnoticed to the stables.

The painting, five panels full, leaned almost vertical below the fading images on the north wall. The boy saw two identical copies, the mother above and slight tilted son below. The Prior did not weep, for he had exhausted his tears at former unveilings, yet the Archbishop was overcome. He froze still, as Brother Filippo had ere, yet neither wept nor collapsed. His speechlessness lasted a quarter hour, stirred out of it only by the stars, who whinnied in agreement. Speechless still and now weeping, the Archbishop walked to the stars and stroked the nose of each one, for they were weaved tight into this miracle.

Then the Archbishop advanced the boy a new plan: tacking the wooden panels upon the flaking north wall would not destroy the original yet might even help preserve it. The boy reflected on this new plan, but again demurred. Though it solved the problem of sin, it made worse the problem of discovery, an insight to which the Archbishop laughingly admitted he had been blinded by his awe.

"How can you, a mere boy, remain in good judgment and nary be blinded with awe?" he asked the boy. The boy knew not in what manner to answer this lofty question, except to venture that awe must be like old grief, it remains there always to see but the feelings can be stored away, and so he said. "Aye," said the Archbishop, "this is a good and wise description."

Upon more discussings, the boy and two men revised their plan for transport, worried that a high stack of connected panels—twice as long as the panel of the legs—might more likely tumble and more likely attract attention. So Brothers Bartolomeo and Filippo detached the panels from another and distributed their packing to five different stars: Canis Minor, Moon, Cancer, Pleiades, and Aquarius, each with pack saddles. The Archbishop upon Canis Major, the Prior upon Orion, Brother Bartolomeo upon Ursa Minor, Brother Filippo upon Ursa Major (the largest star matching the largest rider), and the boy upon Cassiopeia (smallest for smallest) would lead the five pack horses carrying the five miracles.

When the Prior overheard the boy comforting Centaurus and Pisces, the two stars excluded of the historic journey, he advised the boy bring them along, with the excuse that extra horses were always wise. Thusly did the twelve stars, five miracles, one boy, two true monks and two false depart for the city. Only the mule remained in the stables, unlonely in its stupidity.

Brother Filippo was in mild agitation of an attack by the remaining moths, whilst Brother Bartolomeo agitated less mildly of an attack of highwaymen. The Archbishop and the Prior agitated greatly beyond the horizon, to the darkness in Spain. Neither of the Brothers' fears came to pass, and the journey completed without incident. Yet the Spanish darkness loomed.

The boy had former seen the great cathedral on his few travels to the city. None could traverse any portion of the city and not see the cathedral's skyward spires. The pigment shop was near the cathedral's piazza, so the boy twice beheld the majesty of the building whole. Yet now he was entering it, lo entering the most magnificent structure ever his eyes saw.

The majesty inside exceeded the majesty out, both by size and quality. The interiors vaulted by some impossibility higher than the exteriors. The boy's soul soared thrice higher than at the Priory chapels, lofted by the thrice higher arched frescoes. Yet these too merely told of tales of men dressed godly. They did not, as the miracle painting, sing of the gods within the men.

The Archbishop's rectory was larger than the whole of the Priory. He directed the men and boy place the five panels in an airy study already stuffed with artly matters, tapestries, and rugs. The study was larger than the whole of the Priory stables. The Archbishop advised his priests would complete the installation, and after joining the weary expeditioners at table, set special in the massive study, bid them farewell. He rewarded each brother and the boy with a gold coin, and the Prior with a genuine embrace.

"Worry not, my dear Alessandro, the masterpiece is safe here, clothed in the garments of my reflected power. But take care of yourself and this miracle boy, for my power is great only against those who understand it. The madmen in Seville are fury blinded to it, and you and this boy may burn ere my power to douse can bear."

True these warning words turned, and quick, for not two days past the expeditioners' return the gate brothers announced strange black visitors. A column of twelve dark soldiers pointed by a dark bishop awaited entrance. The soldiers of the black fire had arrived from Seville, stoked by the true rantings of the apprentice.

As before, the Prior immediately upon the announcement of the visitors directed Bartolomeo repeat moving the boy and his trappings from stable to root cellar. Then the Prior invited the visitors stable their mounts and the soldiers join the friars at table. Friar Ignacio special welcomed the soldiers with Spanish talking. Brother Filippo led the black steeds into the stables, four-by-four-by-five, where the stars startled great then remained slight uneasy through the visit.

The Prior invited the black bishop dine with him in the Priory, and upon discovering the depth of their gulf in language summoned Friar Ignatius to serve translator, though Ignatius's Italian was hardly better than the Spanish bishop's. The bishop smiled throughout the meal in all circumstances, a strange unhappy smile. He was lance thin, hardly of more heft than the boy himself, and his voice considerable high and shrill. He told he was a judge of the Tribunal of the Holy Office of the Inquisition, commissioned by the Archbishop of Seville himself to make inquiry reports of heresy at this Priory. A boy claimed Godly powers to vision an old dead fresco. The smiling bishop's teeth were black.

When queried the Prior of the black bishop how he might assist, the bishop inquired of the boy's location. Reckoning the apprentice informed the Spaniards true, and if not that Friar Ignacio soon would, the Prior wisely did not repeat his false tales of the boy's insanity and removal. The Prior answered instead that the boy had abandoned the Priory weeks ago, and none knew where he had gone. In parry of further black examination, volunteered the Prior that others had recent inquired of the boy and he told false tales of the boy's madness and French removal only to spare the Church embarrassment. The Prior deep worried that Friar Ignacio had spied the boy in the last few weeks and would disclose this new lie to his countrymen.

The bishop, still black smiling, queried whether he might make special inquiry of the Priory's servants and even friars to confirm the boy gone, by which the Prior knew "special inquiry" oft led to torture. Without response, the bishop continued that he would not think to subject such a well-known Dominican as the Prior himself to special inquiry, and repeated his request to special inquire others.

"Nay," said the Prior standing. "If you are to torture any of my community you shall torture me firstly."

"I do not need your permission. I have twelve soldiers of the Tribunal to enforce my will."

"Yet you have asked my permission," now the Prior smiled.

"I know the boy is here," the Spaniard said, quick glancing at Friar Ignacio. "I suspect him offspring of converso, or worse, and if true he must be executed. But let us not clash swords. Lo, it is beyond Compline. Let us sleep on this juncture of wills, and confer again at Prime."

The instant the black bishop to his room retired, the Prior to the root cellar dashed, once sure that none of the soldiers of the black fire had followed him. He commanded Bartolomeo run to the city to message the Archbishop, and explained the bewildered brother could take no horse nor even the mule, for the black soldiers camped in the stables. Yet firstly Bartolomeo was to waken Brother Filippo and summon him to the root cellar, warning him to sure he was not spied by the soldiers.

At the root cellar the Prior told the frightened Filippo and the unfrightened boy of the black situation. He commanded Filippo sneak unawared into the stables and retrieve two fast horses that the boy and brother might ride unnoticed up to the mountain convent and there await.

"Nay," said the boy, "the stars would stir even at known Filippo, yet I can retrieve them in utter silence." The Prior worried of the boy's life, yet assented, knowing the boy's judgment sound, special with the stars.

The boy proceeded, and whilst the stars obeyed his whispers for silence, not so the thirteen black visitors. Their stirrings in turn stirred the soldiers, and great commotion ensued in foreign words the boy did not understand. As their weapons the soldiers retrieved, and upon their twelve steeds they began to perch, the stars and even the mule bolted from the stables as one, the boy upon Cassiopeia. As the herd passed, Ursa Major paused and Brother Filippo mounted, not without some difficulty.

"After them!" commanded the sergeant in Spanish. Yet the black steeds froze unmoving. The soldiers were general kind to their workmates, kinder sure than to the human objects of their force, thus they did not at first resort to whip. As the frozen moments grew so did the soldiers' impatience, and whip they finally employed. Yet even upon these cruel urgings the steeds would not move, not until boy, brother, stars, and mule were at least a mile onto the mountain road.

Chapter 9

Home

When finally the black mounts returned to senses and soldierly duties, the sergeant inquired of the nearest friar where went the herd of slow workhorses commanded by the boy and trailed by the mule. Had any brother or other friar been so inquired, he would have sent the black soldiers on the road to the city, opposite the true direction. Yet Satan had arranged the object of their inquiry to be Friar Ignacio, who directed them true to the mountain road.

The events following remain in dispute amongst the town and mountain folk. Some say the black steeds slowered the chase by will, permitting the fugitives escape. Yet every soldier in the chase averred there was no slowing, save the beginning stubbornness in the stables. Some say Friar Ignacio led them all astray, yet this is plain false, for the fugitive tracks the soldiers found upon the mountain road.

Some say the stars circled back, went to the city and there enjoyed the protection of the Archbishop. Yet after months of spying, the determined apprentice saw not one nit of proof the absconders were there. And indeed the Archbishop swore by written oath to his Spanish colleague that he was not harboring them, though in more correspondence he refused answer whether he knew what became of them. For know he did, from the reports of the soldiers.

Snow had fallen overnight in the mountains yet was not falling upon the alpine chase, which greatly assisted their pursuit. Also assisting was a full moon, allowing the hunt continue long past Vespers. Followed the black soldiers the snow-pressed tracks up the switching mountain road, past convent orphanage and through unroaded and near vertical forests to the mountain's crest. Followed they down the mountain's side opposite and into an open valley with village and flowing river. Followed they across river into the valley, yet suddenly narrowed the tracks from twelve horses and one mule to a single mule.

Knowing this impossible, the sergeant closer examined the tracks and discovered them not horse tracks at all yet an array of mule tracks. The twelve horses had become twelve mules. Knowing this too impossible, with closer detection the sergeant saw that half the tracks faced away yet half faced returning, from which he reasoned that the wide array was made by the single mule going forward for some distance then returning then repeating until the tracks were twelve wide. Stranger still, so strange he did not share with his men, the sergeant discovered upon his close inspection the shape of these arrayed mule tracks proved the mule was moving at great speed, greater than the gallop of the soldiers' fastest mount.

The sergeant directed they follow these arrayed mule tracks back all the distance to the river. There he discovered the mule-made began on this far bank, but opposite were true horse tracks, ending at the river. From this the sergeant surmised the horses had traversed inside the stream to deceive, the mule complicit in the deception by fashioning the array of false horse prints from the far bank and beyond.

Upon these revelations, the sergeant divided his troops, commanding half pursue the false horse tracks and return to the point where the mule proceeded without trickery, then follow and find the mule. This mule half he ordered commanded by his most senior soldier, also the best-skilled of tracking next only the sergeant himself. The remaining soldiers, under the sergeant's command, would attend to the disappearing horses by surveilling for great distances both riverbanks for their exit.

The commander of those chasing mule made report of its uncommon speed, both in the false array and in the continuing single file, confirming the sergeant's earlier discovery. The shape of the mule's tracks in single file revealed a speed twice the speed of the soldier's steeds at gallop full. "Impossible," said the others, yet when dismounted they too noticed the signs of speed in the mule's snow-pressed hollows, for none was unschooled of tracking. And indeed, followed they at gallop full the mule's lightning markings up out of the valley and cross two mountain ranges and still the speedy prints never appeared joint with their maker.

On the opposite of the second range, the soldiers found a be-fuddled Brother Filippo, half-mad in the snow. Reported he that as the fugitive herd approached the river, the boy commanded him upon the mule, despite his protestations that the tiny creature could never his great weight bear. Filippo reported that the mule not only took the load fine, but that it exploded across the river at such great speed that the poor brother lost all senses, to awake only when the soldiers appeared. The soldiers then surrendered to the setting moon, to their workmates' exhaustions, and to the mystery, return-ing to the Priory with Brother Filippo their only prize.

The soldiers in reconnoit along the river ended even emp-tier, though combed they five miles in each direction and on each bank side. Nowhere in either five-mile length discovered they any signs of river exit by any animal, least a herd of workhorses. The sergeant even inquired of the timid village straddling the river, but all villagers stood in mute fear of the black uniforms. The sergeant did not continue with special inquiry for the darkness commanded his return to the Priory.

With troops reunited there and sergeant communicating with his most senior, discovered they each other's failures. The sergeant then reported these failures to the black bishop, yet did not report the miraculous details of the mule who feigned a herd of horses or galloped as wind. Told he his unhappy leader only that the prey escaped by entering the river, the fat brother falling off in process, and that the darkness of the set moon prevented further chase.

Upon this news the bishop's face continued its darkly smile yet with eyes burned hot. Ordered he the Prior arrested and held in the stables, and his soldiers obeyed, placing the Prior in chains. Following him there after some passing minutes, calculated to grow fear in the prisoner, the black bishop demanded explanation, yet the Prior refused answer and now he selfsame smiled. The black bishop threatened the stake and still the Prior smiled wordless.

Still smiling both men were when the soldiers upon the black bishop's orders constructed a staked pyre in the churchyard. When the pyre was ready for occupation and alighting, a period quick short for the soldiers were well-learned in the tools of making the black fires, the Spanish bishop inquired the Prior lastly for explanation. "Tell where be the boy and spare you I this painful death. Faith, I have seen hundreds claim serenity anchored far deeper than yours, then serenity flee cowardly upon the torch." All these threats Friar Ignacio faithfully translated, not without some brightenings of joy.

The Prior remained silent, and to the ready stake the black bishop ordered him. As the soldiers led the Prior out of the stable doors and toward the pyre, commotions at the gate commanded all the men's attentions. It was the Archbishop, riding without escort save Bartolomeo. The Archbishop dismounted, spied the staked pyre and his chained friend and demanded explanation, the demand and response translated by now worried Friar Ignacio.

The black Spaniard replied in snarling smile that the Archbishop had nay power either to demand explanation or interfere, for his was the remit of the Tribunal of the Holy Office of the Inquisition. The Archbishop of Milan, said further the Spaniard through Friar Ignacio, was at best of equal with the Archbishop of Seville, and thusly had no commanding authority over Seville's deputation.

The Archbishop like lightning drew sword from under robes and placed its point upon the black bishop's neck ere any soldiers could draw. "Have you forgotten who I am, you Spanish beetle? Have your men forgotten? Nay, they do not know, do they? You have not told them. Let us educate." These words Ignacio was far frightened to make into Spanish, yet the black bishop understood.

Now speaking to the soldiers in Spanish yet holding still the sword point for killing, keeping his eyes on the point whilst turning his mitred head slight to the soldiers, the Archbishop said, "My name is Constantino Odescalchi, and I am younger brother to Benedetto Odescalchi. Know you that name? My brother's churchly appellation is Innocent XI." All the black soldiers, friars, and brothers genuflected and kneeled to the shared blood of His Holiness. Addressing back to the black bishop, said the Archbishop, "I could run you through and be heroed in Rome. The days of this Spanish plague are over, my brother His Holiness Innocent XI will see to it."

The Archbishop ordered the black sergeant arrest his own bishop, and the sergeant obeyed eager, as did his men, for none greatly loved the too brutal little man despight their own willing brutality, and detained they their former commander in the root cellar. The Prior then invited the black sergeant and all his soldiers to table in the Priory, where the Archbishop and the Prior heard of the true events of the chase, of the disappearing stars and the john mule making false wide horse tracks and running swift as wind.

The Prior threw back his head at this tale, told by the sergeant and translated by the Archbishop, laughing hearty at the stupid mule's clever diversions. Holding aloft his wine glass, proposed the Prior a toast to the gentle creature thusly: "To the sweet mule, for whom we need not pray God's speed for of this quality the gentle beast be already possessed," to which all laughed great once translated, "yet we pray for its wellness, that it come finally to a peaceful rest, and that its soul join someday its stable stars." Of this salute all at table joined with loud hurrahs, including the Archbishop.

The Archbishop then told the soldiers the full tale of the boy and the stars and the copied masterpiece painting, swearing them not tell their bishop. He said these matters firstly in Spanish then in

Italian, for the Prior's understanding. The Prior concerned at this vouchsafing, yet the Archbishop was secure in his judgment of the soldiers' good and even more secure in the protections of his own considerable familial powers, and urged the Prior peace.

Responding to this tale of wonder, with the Archbishop again translating, the sergeant expressed great sadness at the absence of the miracle boy and his stars, and worried deep where they became. Begged he the Prior's and Archbishop's forgiveness for driving boy and herd away, and offered he and his men renew the search.

"Nay," said the Archbishop, "boy, stars, and mule, all are safe home."

The Archbishop mercifully dispatched the black bishop and his soldiers to Seville, with orders the soldiers respect the bishop's station and treat him in all ways their liege, save they would do no acts of special inquiry nor otherwise but return directly home. The Archbishop gave to the sergeant a sealed message for his churchly comrade in Seville, directing its seal not be vouchsafed to any but he. This message was the aforementioned oath that the Archbishop was not in harbor of the missing boy.

It later came to be learned that so reproachful the black bishop was to his men for their disloyalty in his arrest, and so frequent threatened he them with torture and death upon return, they murdered him near Pavia, and fled service. The loyal sergeant, not part of the sedition, tied they in ropes for their escape, abling him when loosened to deliver the sealed message to the Archbishop of Seville.

Much distressed was the great Spanish churchman at the Italian treatment of his deputation, and uncalmed by the Archbishop of Milan's written oath. Yet powerless the Spaniard was against this renegade brother of His Holiness, particular after the renegade did in two years don red cap and trek to the bosom of physical protections in Rome. Even those protections would not have been sufficient against the powers of the Spanish King, yet the Spanish King wielded them not, for his fondness of the Archbishop of Seville was never great, and certain fell far short to spend the coin of power on such trivials.

Nay reports of the copied masterpiece did ever make text, yet a handful of Dominicans reported with words unwrit that the new cardinal's caravan to Rome packed a secreted cargo of five large wooden panels. These rumors continued that the mystery wood delivered to the Cardinal's spacious apartment in Rome. Some said they contained the boards from the Christ's birth manger, others the true walls of the Virgin Mary's house. All these words, untexted, like water dried and vanished with time.

The Prior, the worldly sailor less befaithed of regular miracle than his old friend, commissioned investigation into the fate of the boy and stars and mule. Inquired he deeply of Brother Filippo, who repeated the truth told to the soldiers of his senses lost upon the galloping mule. Many of the rivered villagers, no drunks or blind among them, swore of the fugitive horses leaping at water's edge, the boy upon the smallest mare, and landing all of them in the sky, each making different twinklings. One of these villagers averred one of the twinklings on the moon itself. Yet others saw nay horses running least soaring least populating the heavens.

The examinations of the mule's fate were likewise frayed. One shepherd boy from the river village oathed he witnessed a mule trekking back and forth for hundreds of yards at the west bank, galloping as a steed seized with madness, and even counted the mule making twelve separate travels to and fro across the snow fast as falcon hunting mice. Alpine villagers north swore of a donkey running up mountain trails deep in snow yet float-ing atop, and travelling with more haste than the fastest chamois. Others, in valleys and mountains, saw naught.

Regular the Prior travelled to the city with Brothers Bar-tolomeo and Filippo whilst his friend still bishoped there, to see the great copied masterpiece. And once friend became cardinal, thrice to Rome the Prior voyaged with Filippo, for poor Bar-tolomeo's soul by then had risen. Three times Prior and Brother, sailor and blacksmith, lay their eyes upon the miracle. In their ending years, too frail for travel, the two daily raised the study tapestry to gaze upon the feet, to remember the face attached and the boy who painted them, and to weep.

The Cardinal whilom Archbishop served Rome well and humbly. When died his brother after more a decade in highest service, many rumors churned his brother would succeed yet it did nary come to pass. Twin rumors spun of a miracle painting brought he from Milan, yet these too never bloomed real.

The Cardinal built for his resting a fine mausoleum in the outskirts of Rome. Though built of marbles and stones imported afar, commissioned he from carpenters sworn to secrecy a pine sarcophagus made with five large panels, four for sides and one for top with a stone bottom. To keep vermin and rot away, directed he that the rough exterior wood be sealed with a special painter's tincture, and that the whole coffin be covered with stones from a small priory near west of Milan. When opined his chief carpenter that the tincture and stones would not prevent his body's decay, said the Cardinal, "The thing preserved will not be my body."

Neither he, his brother, nor his brother's successor victored over the excesses in Spain, yet many say their efforting rounded its worst edges. Not until the Spanish royal power fully set did Seville's.

The Prior followed his old sailing friend in death. He died in penury, having through his aging spent the whole of his fortune in goodly church endeavors, which included enlarging the convent orphanage so that the eldering boys' fate of exclusion, and commissioning into the moths, could be some delayed. In the same year of the Prior's death, on the day of the Feast of St. Francis of Assisi, Brother Filippo died sleeping.

Both men buried in the Priory graveyard aside Bartolomeo, the Prior's shell marked with a fine stone carving and the two Brothers' with finely carved oaken crosses. The aged Brothers Vincenzo and Stefano, the selfsame drunk and blind witnesses to the miracle rescuers of the boy and his stars, reported to the new Prior that each night for ten following the Feast of St. Francis witnessed they a small mule visit the three graves.